DEATH
OF A
GUNSLINGER

DEATH
OF A
GUNSLINGER

•

HOWARD PELHAM

AVALON BOOKS
THOMAS BOUREGY AND COMPANY, INC.
401 LAFAYETTE STREET
NEW YORK, NEW YORK 10003

34309178

PRINTED IN THE UNITED STATES OF AMERICA
ON ACID-FREE PAPER
BY HADDON CRAFTSMEN, SCRANTON, PENNSYLVANIA

For Jessica Perry Onesty,
whose helpful reactions
made this a better novel.

Chapter One

"Your pa's coming to Abilene," Uncle Ben said.

The three of us—me, Aunt Mamie, and Uncle Ben—were at the supper table. We were about finished eating, and my guess is that Uncle Ben had saved that news till we'd had our supper.

Pa was Aunt Mamie's brother, and he hadn't been back to Abilene since he dropped me off for Aunt Mamie and Uncle Ben Martin to care for. I was two then.

I didn't know what to think or say. I guess that's the way you feel when you haven't heard a word from your pa in eleven years and don't know what he looks like except from seeing him in a picture.

The lamp that sat in the middle of the table had yet to be lighted, and the kitchen was filling with shadows. I had to look hard to see how Aunt Mamie was taking the news. There was some conflict in her face.

Wyatt Walker, my pa, was her only brother, and there was that basic rule in her that you loved and were loyal to blood kin, though you didn't approve of what they did, and she certainly didn't approve of what Pa had done. He had killed several men by then.

Aunt Mamie was older than Pa—past forty, I think, though she never told me her age. Of medium height, she had begun to put on weight. It gave her a plump, comfortable look. She had brown hair, which she wore long, but most of the time it was wound into a ball and pinned at the nape of her neck. She had a few strands of gray, but she didn't seem to mind—certainly, Uncle Ben didn't.

"When, Ben?" Aunt Mamie asked.

"Tomorrow," he said. "I got a telegram at the store this afternoon. Said he was coming into Abilene on horseback. Why, he must be within twenty miles of us this minute."

Uncle Ben was a short, wiry man—a little shorter than Aunt Mamie. But he made up for that with a ramrod-straight back and shoulders that he kept permanently squared. He had retained that stature from his days in the Army where he was a captain. But all that stiffness was just show. Once you got to know him you found out he was one of the kindest men you'd want to know.

The kindness was there in his face. He had smile wrinkles about his mouth that softened his otherwise blunt features. He had permanent wrinkles extending out from his eyes from squinting into a hot Kansas sun in summer and across the white snows in winter. Though he was older than Aunt Mamie, his auburn hair hadn't a hint of gray in it, and the gleam in his gray-green eyes looked younger still.

"Why couldn't he have just come in the train?" Aunt Mamie asked. "We would have known when to expect him. We could have met him and made him welcome."

I waited for Uncle Ben to answer, but I knew why he hadn't. Mr. Gilpin, the telegrapher, would have spread the word. Everyone in Abilene would have turned out.

"He wanted to avoid a crowd, I think," Uncle Ben said.

Aunt Mamie hadn't thought of that. She didn't concentrate on Pa's fame or the things he had done to achieve it. Mostly, she liked to remember when they were growing up. She agreed with Rev. Todd Baker, the minister, that men who carried guns, gambled, and messed with bad women were apt to wind up in hell.

I thought of little else but his present life, however, not having known him in any other time. I kept up with all the stories about him. For instance, there was his latest episode, the Kennedy killings. He had recently killed two of three Kennedy brothers down in El Paso. The paper ran that on the front page. Some folks were saying it would maybe become his most famous gunfight.

The Kennedys wanted the whole bar in some saloon for themselves. They ordered Pa to leave and told him what they'd do if he didn't. It's possible they were out to add to their reputations and knew exactly who he was. Anyway, it was the wrong thing for them to try.

When the smoke cleared, two Kennedys were bloodying the sawdust floor . . . dead. The other, the oldest, whose name was Lafe, managed to crawl from the saloon. Folks told Pa he better follow and finish Lafe off, that Lafe Kennedy would never rest till he had killed the man who had shot down his brothers.

But Pa let him go. He just reloaded his six-gun, walked back to the bar, lifted the drink, and tossed it down.

The marshal came and said good riddance when he was told what had happened. As for Lafe, he crawled off somewhere and wasn't heard from till his wounds healed. Then he sent word to Pa that he'd get him if it was the last thing he ever did.

Lafe had already tried once. He had recruited some men into a gang, trailed after Pa, tried to ambush him, and failed. Lafe announced that he wouldn't fail a second time.

Lafe Kennedy's gang was said to be a rowdy bunch. Rumor had it that the members were some of the most feared names in the West, killers all. Waiting for the next episode was like waiting for the next installment in one of those adventure stories the paper sometimes runs. I couldn't wait to hear, and it concerned my pa, though Wyatt Walker didn't seem like a pa to me.

We had been silent for a while at the supper table. I reckon each of us was busy with his own thoughts as to what Wyatt Walker might be coming to Abilene for. As for me, one of my first thoughts was to wonder if Lafe Kennedy would follow him to Abilene. For some reason the idea made me nervous. I didn't want all of Abilene to see Wyatt Walker shot down if Lafe Kennedy and his gang cornered him in the town.

"Why do you think he decided to come home, Ben?" Aunt Mamie asked.

"Don't know," Uncle Ben said. "He didn't say in the telegram . . . just that we could expect him tomorrow."

Aunt Mamie was going through the possibilities in her mind. Then she looked at me.

"Wes, don't you have some chores you didn't finish?" she asked.

"No, ma'am. I done them all."

"Did, son, *did* them all." Then: "I saw you feed my hens, but did you water them?"

"Yes, ma'am."

"Still, maybe you should check the water again. Hens get awful thirsty along about nighttime. You go out there and see if they've finished off their water. They might not lay their eggs tomorrow if they go to roost thirsty."

I'd never heard of anything like that before. I knew she hadn't, either. She never fibbed like that unless she was a little desperate to get me out of the way. Pushing back from the table, I went out the back door, but I stopped just around the corner of the house where I could hear clearly what was being said inside.

The time was early June, and the sun was about to go down. Above the horizon, red-bellied clouds caught the last of the daylight. A mockingbird settled on a limb of the chinaberry tree and began to sing.

"He's coming home for Wesley, ain't he, Ben?" Aunt Mamie asked.

Her question surprised me. In none of my thoughts of Wyatt Walker, even when I thought of him as my pa, had it ever crossed my mind that he might one day ride into Abilene and say "I've come for my son." I had daydreamed of adventure, but none of my dreams had ever been about me riding off to live with Wyatt Walker. Now the notion that he might be coming to Abilene for me was enough to set my head spinning.

Then Uncle Ben said, "I don't think we should jump to any conclusions, wife. Right now only your brother knows why he's coming to Abilene."

"I just don't know what I'd do if we lost the boy," Aunt Mamie said. "He's like the son we never had. Maybe I even love him more, because I couldn't have my own. I just thank God every day that Wyatt chose to leave him with us when Sue Ellen died."

Sue Ellen was my ma. She was a very beautiful woman and much loved by Pa. I never really knew what Aunt Mamie thought of her. She never did say, but I had suspected for a couple of years that there might have been something about Sue Ellen Aunt Mamie disapproved of.

"Tell me you won't let Wyatt take him away, Ben," she added.

I have to tell you the softest place in my heart was reserved for Aunt Mamie. In all those years I don't remember ever getting a harsh word from her. When I got in trouble in school—which I did often enough, not being the scholarly type—Aunt Mamie had a way of understanding what was going on in my head. She didn't condone it—she didn't condone what Pa had done either—but she didn't judge a fella. She had a power over you, though, a power that she didn't seem to know about. It sprang from the unqualified love she gave, whether you deserved it or not.

I could hear the fear in her voice when she thought she might lose me, and I wanted to go back inside, hug her, and promise I'd never leave her.

Then I thought of what I'd be missing if Wyatt Walker was coming to Abilene for me, and I was caught between the excitement of that and the guilt from even the thought that I would go off with someone like Wyatt Walker and leave Aunt Mamie and Uncle Ben.

Then, in the tenderest voice I think I ever heard, Uncle Ben said, "Maybe you should consider that it's the boy he's coming for, Mamie. He has the legal right, and it ain't natural for a man to go on living away from his own flesh and blood."

"Maybe he's coming to Abilene to settle down," she said. "Yes, maybe that's it. As you say, it isn't natural for a man to live away from his own flesh and blood, but it isn't natural, either, for him to continue in the kind of life he's led since Sue Ellen died."

"He couldn't come here and settle down, Mamie."

"Why ever not? Abilene is a nice town. I see it changing every day. Why couldn't Wyatt come here and begin to live a sensible kind of life?"

"Mamie . . . the kind of man he is . . . you know, the notorious gunslinger kind. Well, men like that just aren't allowed to settle down and live like ordinary people. They have that reputation, and there are men who are crazy to build their reputations by calling men like Wyatt out. No, Wyatt won't be able to settle down in Abilene or anywhere else he's known. But maybe he just wants to see the boy. After all, having a thirteen-year-old boy tagging along would cramp his style when it comes to all those big poker games we're always hearing about."

"But what if he *has* come for him, Ben? What if he has?"

"Well then, there ain't nothing we can do. He has the legal right."

There was silence from the kitchen, but I could feel what was going on. It seemed to seep through the wall. I told myself to go in there and tell them that it made no difference what Wyatt Walker was coming to Abilene for—that if it was for me, he was making the trip for nothing.

"You reckon he's over Sue Ellen by now?" Aunt Mamie asked. "I never saw a man more filled with grief than Wyatt was when he brought the boy to us. Seemed to me like he didn't care if he lived or not. Yes, time has healed his heart, and whether you believe he can or not, he's going to make an effort to settle down."

The last hint of red had now vanished from the clouds. Darkness was closing in fast to the chorus of crickets and locusts and the whir of a bullbat's wings as he dove overhead. The mockingbird was quiet, and overhead some stars had come out.

I thought of the picture on Aunt Mamie's bureau of Sue Ellen and Wyatt Walker. It was made on the day they were married, capturing them in the mood of a moment long before I was born. I could tell from the picture how happy they were. Sue Ellen was tall and willowy with soft-looking dark hair falling from beneath a wide floppy hat, her eyes widely spaced, the brows a thin dark line above them. She wore a dark suit whose hem came almost to the tops of the patent leather, high-topped shoes. Beneath the suit she wore a white blouse, and at her throat a brooch. A beautiful woman—and happy. Yet there was something sad in the face as well, as though she might have guessed what was in store for her.

I remember when I learned how Sue Ellen died. I must have been about six. There was a prayer Aunt Mamie had taught me, asking God to look after us all, including Wyatt Walker and, of course, Sue Ellen, who was now dead and living with the angels.

"How did she die?" I asked when the prayer was finished.

"She and your pa were out riding. They decided to race. Her horse fell and pitched her. Her poor neck was broken."

For a long time after that I prayed that God would not only take care of her in heaven but would put her neck back together as well.

Pa is handsome in that picture. He wears a dark suit, a white shirt, and a black string bowtie. He holds a homburg in the crook of his right arm. It gives him a jaunty look. His hair, dark and wavy, is parted in the middle. His brows are dark heavy arches over dark, deep-set eyes. The nose is straight and long, and the smile displays an even row of teeth. The jaws and chin are squared and firm-looking. In fact, Wyatt Walker's face greatly resembles that of John Wilkes Booth, the actor who shot and killed President Lincoln.

Not having anything more than shadowy memories of either Sue Ellen or Wyatt, the way they were in that picture was the way I always thought of them. They were two beautiful strangers, about as real to me as characters from some story.

Aunt Mamie and Uncle Ben were still talking.

"Maybe he's got over Sue Ellen's death," Uncle Ben said. "I reckon we'll just have to wait till he gets here and see. And maybe he will have come for Wes, and if he has, there is something you should consider."

"What?"

"Even if he isn't coming for Wes this time, he will sooner or later. Or maybe it'll be Wes wanting to go to him. We'd make enemies of them both if we tried to stand between them when that day comes. And there is something else, wife. In his present state Wyatt Walker is a lost soul. I've heard you say it many times, heard you wonder what it was that could bring him to a better life. Well, maybe it's his son. Maybe if the boy was with him, Wyatt could return to the man he once was. Have you ever thought of that?"

"I've thought of it, Ben. Lord knows, I've thought of it a lot, but if the time ever comes, it'll hurt."

The sound in her voice about broke my heart. I stood up and went inside. "The hens had plenty of water," I said.

"Thank you anyway, Wesley, and I didn't offer you

a piece of pie before I sent you out. Would you like it now?"

"I guess I'll just go to bed," I said.

My turning down pie was so unusual that Aunt Mamie stood up and was about to come around the table to take my temperature, but Uncle Ben put a hand up and stopped her.

Of course, I wasn't sleepy. I just had all these things to think about. Could I leave Aunt Mamie and Uncle Ben behind if Wyatt Walker was coming to town for me? I fought that question for some time before I could sleep.

Chapter Two

I was on the front porch most of the next day looking for him. I was still wrestling with myself, and it hadn't helped much that Aunt Mamie couldn't seem to keep her hands off me during breakfast. Not that I minded, if touching me helped to ease her thoughts.

In an effort to make the day pass a little faster I kept telling myself that it was no use being so worked up. Taking me away with him might not be the reason Wyatt Walker was coming to Abilene at all, but it didn't help. Nothing would till he arrived and said right out why he had come.

But something strange began to happen inside me that day too. I began to wonder more than I ever had about why he had stayed away so long. I had heard all about his love for my ma, of course, and how I would have been a reminder of her for him, but none of that seemed sufficient reason for a pa staying so long away from his son. I hadn't thought much about that before, since Aunt Mamie and Uncle Ben seemed more like my ma and pa than some handsome stranger in a picture who was always getting into gunfights.

Then I began to get mad, and it wasn't Wyatt Walker, the stranger, I was mad at. It was my pa, the man who had dropped me off eleven years before and been gone ever since.

A boy's pa, I kept telling myself, shouldn't have done such a thing, and for the first time I felt a lot of resentment that he had stayed away from me all that time. Well, I said to myself, if he thinks he can just ride in and make things all right, he'll discover how wrong that is.

He turned in from the east running road that continued on to Kansas City, riding up the long, narrow, cottonwood-lined road that led up to the house. It was late in the afternoon, and the bit of dust kicked up by the big black horse looked almost red in the hazel light.

He looked bigger than life on that black horse, and he was leading a second horse, more yellow than red, a color some call claybank. In the beginning I mistook the second horse for a pack animal, but when they were nearer, I saw that the horse carried nothing more than a new-looking empty saddle.

I remember thinking I should get up and go inside and tell Aunt Mamie and Uncle Ben that he was here. I couldn't seem to move, though. I just sat there and watched him ride into the yard on that high-stepping black horse.

He pulled up before the house, but he didn't step down. He was waiting to be asked; it was the custom for strangers.

We looked each other over, him on that black horse and me in a rocking chair I had just about worn out waiting for him.

I wanted to say something, but when I opened my mouth to speak, my throat was so dry and sticky I couldn't make a sound. He didn't seem able to talk, either, or if he could he chose not to.

He didn't resemble at all the dark handsome man in

the picture. Maybe he was a worn, older version of that man, but I wasn't even sure of that. The way the weakening sun struck his face might have had something to do with it. Its reddish tint pointed up the paleness of his face and made the dark eyes look a whole lot bigger. There were some wrinkles too, not like those in Uncle Ben's face, good wrinkles from smiling a lot and looking pleasurably off into a bright Kansas sun. These were troubling wrinkles, wrinkles that didn't come from happy thoughts.

He wasn't dressed right, either. Instead of the dark suit, white shirt, and the homburg, he wore a pair of faded denims, a faded blue shirt, and dusty boots. And I couldn't keep my eyes from the big gun he wore on his hip, a Colt .45, not a fancy gun like gunslingers are supposed to wear.

What I could see of the barrel, though, told me it was well kept, for it was clean and polished. Its handles were brown bone and the bone was shiny, but more from use than anything else. His gunbelt was filled with cartridges, and they were so fresh and clean-looking they glinted in the fast-fading light. In fact, except for the way the gun rested so securely on his hip, and the sense of vitality and power that seemed to seep out from him to me, Wyatt Walker might have passed for some aging cowboy.

He had come all the way from Texas, but to me it seemed he had come a lot farther—all the way from a world I knew nothing about, certainly a different one than I knew in Abilene.

Suddenly, he took his hat off, doing it slowly, deliberately, a wide-brimmed Stetson whose brim was rolled up on either side, and he said, "You must be Wesley."

He waited for me to speak, but I still couldn't, and then Aunt Mamie said from behind me, "Wyatt, is it really you? Is it?"

He seemed to get a little choked up, and then he said, "It's me, Sister."

I was embarrassed at the sudden raw emotion in his face, and I turned and looked at Aunt Mamie. She had stopped a few steps back on the porch, her hands clasped to her heart in a gesture of thanksgiving, and she looked as if she had just landed in heaven.

I heard the creak of leather and turned back to look at Wyatt Walker. He was swinging down. He hit the ground and then walked up to the steps, climbed them, and stood before Aunt Mamie. Suddenly, they were in each other's arms, and I could hear Aunt Mamie sobbing like she had never cried before, and there was a lump in my throat so big I couldn't swallow.

"Dearest, dearest Wyatt! You've come home at last!" Then she turned her face toward heaven, though there was only the roof of the porch up there, and she said, "Dear God, you've answered my prayers, and I thank you."

His face was well above her head, and though the light was dimmer now, I thought I saw a slight quiver of his features, like the first tremor of a cliff about to cave in.

They stepped back from each other, and he said, "I've wanted to come, Mamie. I've thought about it for some time, but some things stood in the way."

"You don't have to explain to me, Wyatt. You never did, you know. I'm just happy you're here at last. Ben and Wes are happy, too. Aren't you happy, Wesley?" she asked, turning to me.

But I still couldn't talk, and if I'd been able, I doubt I could have thought of anything to say.

Uncle Ben stood framed in the doorway. He stepped out onto the porch and extended a hand. "You're welcome here, Wyatt, *truly* welcome. I hope you know that."

They shook, and Wyatt Walker said, "That means a lot to me, Ben. I wasn't sure, you know, after all the business of . . ." He let it trail off.

"You're still family to us, Wyatt."

"Thank you, Ben."

There was some awkward silence then, and though he wasn't looking at me, I had this strong feeling I was on Wyatt Walker's mind. He was certainly on mine, this worn, tired-looking man who didn't seem as tall in person as he had always looked in that picture.

And despite the way he looked, the anger that had been building in me all that day got stronger still, and I wanted to say something that would let him know what a pa should feel after he'd been away from his only son so many years. But maybe something wiser than I was at the time took over and kept me from talking.

Then Aunt Mamie broke the silence. "This is Wesley, Wyatt. This is your son. Wesley, say hello to your father."

We looked at each other again across an eleven-year chasm. I could feel my face growing hot. That made me madder still, because the last thing I wanted to show was that it mattered to me any at all that he had finally come home. The muscles in his face twitched a couple of times as he stood there and looked at me.

Aunt Mamie broke in again. "Stand up, Wes. Stand

up so your father can take a good look at you. He wants to see how much you've grown—don't you, Wyatt?''

That was a silly thing for her to say, since I had been two the last time he saw me, and probably not as tall as his arm was long.

''I surely do, Mamie . . . Wes,'' he said, and there was a crack in his voice that seemed to suggest the sides of *his* throat had hardened up.

I stood up, and he took a couple of steps toward me, his hand out. I didn't want to take it, but the desire to please Aunt Mamie was strong. We shook.

My knees were weak, and there seemed to be a knot in the pit of my stomach. I could hear myself breathing as well.

''Wesley, I . . .'' He didn't seem able to go on for a moment or so, but then he did. ''Wesley, it's good to see you at last.'' Just that and nothing more.

''Yes, sir,'' I managed.

''Are you hungry, Wyatt?'' Aunt Mamie asked, and she spoke the words a little too loud.

''Starving,'' he said, and he seemed suddenly a little more animated, more cheerful.

''How about some fried chicken and mashed potatoes? That was always your favorite. The chicken is ready and warming, but I left the potatoes to do till you got here. I wanted them to be fresh and fluffy.''

''And there'll be gravy for those potatoes, I expect,'' he said.

''Oh, a whole bowlful.''

''And some pie?''

''Apple.''

I knew then what Aunt Mamie had been doing in the kitchen all afternoon. She'd been fixing this special meal for him. Suddenly, I was jealous. I didn't like the thought of her doing all that for him. I didn't like it at all.

"I've eaten pie all over the West, Sister," he said, "but I never tasted any to measure up to yours and Ma's. The Walker women were always the best pastry cooks in the country."

Somehow what he said made me feel a little cold, for it told of a time between the two of them that I had no experience of, like the feeling I had when I looked at the picture of him and Sue Ellen. Strangely, I found myself wondering why I'd never felt like that when Aunt Mamie talked of those days to me.

Aunt Mamie laughed, laughter that seemed to wash away the years, and Wyatt Walker smiled as well, and suddenly his face didn't seem so wrinkled and worn, and he shed a little of the image of a man coming in from the darkness.

"Ben, you and Wes entertain Wyatt out here on the porch, where it's cool, while I go inside and finish getting supper ready. Wes, you tell your father about how well you've done in school. He's a good student, Wyatt, this son of yours."

I don't know where she got that, but my Aunt Mamie was always one who could put the best face on anything. She went inside, leaving the three of us alone.

"Take that rocker, Wyatt," Uncle Ben said, pointing to the chair next to the one I had been sitting in.

Uncle Ben took the next one over, and I sat again in the one I had been frozen in when Wyatt Walker rode up. We sat there for a moment, the three of us, and the wind suddenly picked up and whipped around the corner of the house, sweeping before it a few yellowing leaves from the chinaberry tree. A rooster crowed from the chicken yard as if to tell us the day was gone.

"That's a fine-looking black horse, Wyatt," Uncle Ben said. "And the claybank looks almost as good."

"I brought the claybank for the boy," he said.

I resented him calling me "boy." Somehow it seemed to emphasize all those years he had been away. For a moment hate welled up in me, or I think it was hate. At least, it was a strong feeling, a little like what I had for Josh Hatton, the school bully, who made a habit of bloodying my nose every week or so.

"Well, let's have a look," Uncle Ben said, and the two of them got up and went down the steps to the horses and circled them.

I just sat there.

Wyatt Walker looked back up at me. "Don't you want to take a look at your horse, Wes?"

"My name is Wesley," I said, my eyes boring into his with as much resentment as I could get into them.

He returned my gaze, and his gaze didn't waver. In those eyes I suddenly thought I saw the man of the gun-fight stories. They weren't cold as they met my gaze, but I was suddenly aware of just how cold they might become had there been real cause.

"I know what your name is," he said. "I'm the one who gave it to you."

"Then use it. Don't be calling me 'boy' no more."

"Wes!" Uncle Ben scolded. "This is your pa you're talking to!"

"Leave him be, Ben. He was right to correct me." Then, turning to me, he continued, "I won't call you 'boy' no more if I can think not to, and now will you come down here and tell me what you think of this clay-bank horse?''

''I reckon I will.''

The truth was, I was about dying to get down there and look at the horse. Till then I'd never had a horse of my own, and it was something I'd wanted mighty bad. I think Uncle Ben would have bought me one if I'd asked him, but I never had.

I couldn't help but feel I'd won some kind of victory as I went down the steps. I felt good about that.

The sun was down now, but enough twilight remained for me to take in the claybank. He was gelded and not quite grown. The mane had a slightly red cast to its black, as did the tail, and the legs above the hooves were shaded black, which merged into the claybank color higher up. There was a white star in his forehead, and as I stood there looking into a pair of brown eyes, he reached out and gave me a nudge with his nose. The tears had been close all along. Now they seeped into my eyes, and I was glad it was dark.

''Here, give him this,'' Wyatt Walker said, and he offered me a lump of sugar.

I took it and offered it to the horse. He lifted it off my fingers, his lips moist and warm, and . . . well, I fell in love with him then and there. I wanted to put my arms about his neck and hold his face to mine, but I held back.

''Thank you,'' I managed, happy I could say anything at all.

''You're welcome,'' he said, and for a moment I thought he was about to call me 'son,' but he didn't. And maybe it was just a feeling I had. Maybe for a moment there I wanted him to say it.

''He is a beauty, Wyatt,'' Uncle Ben said. ''Maybe as

fine as the black when he's grown. You take care of this claybank, Wes,'' he said to me, ''and you'll be as well mounted as any man in Abilene.''

''We should put the horses away,'' Wyatt Walker said to me. ''If you'll lead the way with the claybank, I'll follow along with the black.''

''I'll wait for the two of you on the porch,'' Uncle Ben said, obviously giving Wyatt Walker a chance to be alone with me.

I felt again the claybank nudging my back as I led the way. I sensed as well that I held a vast advantage over Wyatt Walker. I was smart enough to know it came from his guilt for having deserted me.

''You know a man should always see to his horse before he sets down to his own meal,'' Wyatt Walker said from behind me.

That was something I knew, and his saying it seemed forced. But I asked him why that was, and I believe the fact we walked in darkness was the reason I could pretend.

''It's what men learned,'' he said. ''In certain . . . situations, situations you're quite unused to here in Abilene. But in some places a man's life can depend on the care he gives his horse.''

''Like you getting away from Lafe Kennedy?'' I asked.

He was walking along behind me, and he stopped. The darkness seemed to close in a little tighter about me, and I stopped too.

''How is it you know about Lafe Kennedy?'' And his voice seemed to distance out from me, though he was only the length of the claybank back.

''Everyone in Abilene knows about him,'' I said.

"They know about the shootout in El Paso and how you killed his brothers. They know he recruited a gang and ambushed you. They don't know how you got away, though. Was it the black horse?"

"Mostly it was him," he said.

We stood there in the darkness, and it was now so black I couldn't see him.

"Do they talk to you about the gunfights?" he asked.

"Sometimes."

"How does it make you feel?"

"I don't know. Is Lafe Kennedy still after you? Will he follow you to Abilene?"

He didn't answer. I couldn't see him, but I could feel him staring off into the night.

"Let's get on to the barn," he said, and he sounded like a man who was mighty tired.

I wondered why we couldn't talk about it and said so.

"We will, but another time."

I led the way on to the barn.

Chapter Three

Aunt Mamie's supper was special. A great platter of fried chicken sat in the middle of the table. Beside the chicken was a plate of crusty brown biscuits. There were mashed potatoes and gravy, turnip greens plucked fresh from the garden that very day, and coffee or buttermilk.

A cozy picture it was, the four of us seated around the table, the lamplight flickering across the faces as a breeze drifted in through the kitchen door. There was the smell of all that good food, and the occasional clink of fork or knife as we ate.

But the situation was different from when just the three of us sat to eat. Still, there was an unspoken excitement.

There was little talk as we ate. When the pie plates were cleared away, we sat there fiddling with napkins. Aunt Mamie was so nervous she forgot to scold me for being fidgety. Uncle Ben tried several spots along the side of the table before he finally found one where his hands were comfortable.

"I guess it's time I got into why I've come," Wyatt Walker finally said.

Uncle Ben cleared his throat and said, "Makes no difference to us, Wyatt, no difference at all. We're just happy to have you with us."

That was a white lie, of course, but even Aunt Mamie agreed with him.

"That's true, Brother," she said.

There was a silence and then Wyatt Walker began to talk. "I spoke earlier of wanting to come back for a long time, but I just couldn't. It wasn't just the things I've been doing, either."

"What was it then, Wyatt?" Aunt Mamie asked.

Wyatt Walker looked at me. Then he looked down at the table. He scratched a restless hand across his cheek, and I could hear the corns in his hand scrubbing across his beard.

"Seemed to me like the only thing I couldn't do was to come back to a place where I had been with . . . Sue Ellen."

His face had turned into a mask, and his voice was now so low I had to lean forward to hear him. The face didn't show it, but beneath the mask I could feel a terrible emotion.

I didn't know much about the love between a man and a woman, but I'd had to read about Romeo and Juliet in school. I never did understand why the two of them killed themselves. I got a little mad at them because they didn't stay alive and try to work things out. And here was Wyatt Walker, my pa, talking about loving Sue Ellen so much that when she died he couldn't stand to be in a place where they'd been together. I didn't know whether to believe that or not. I thought maybe he was lying, and something else had kept him away.

Uncle Ben must have believed it. He pushed his chair back, got up, and brought the chair around to sit beside Aunt Mamie. Their hands disappeared, and I knew they had them locked together beneath the table.

Wyatt Walker had stopped talking, either because Uncle Ben had moved or because he found he couldn't go on, and there was another long, awkward silence.

"I reckon you had better tell us why you've come, Wyatt," Uncle Ben finally said.

Wyatt Walker shifted in his chair, looked at me again, and said, "Wes there told me you know about Lafe Kennedy. Well, I can't guarantee he's not on my trail. In fact, I have to believe he is, so maybe I should tell you I didn't come here to stay. I'll be leaving in the morning."

"Oh, Wyatt!" Aunt Mamie said and something like a sob escaped her.

"I'd . . . I'd like to stay, Mamie, but I might be putting all of you in danger. I can't do that, but maybe there will come a time when I can return and stay longer. I will hope so anyway."

"Me too, Brother. Me too."

I recalled what Uncle Ben had said about the riffraff that would come crowding in if word got out that Wyatt Walker was in Abilene, so there was that danger as well as the danger of Lafe Kennedy showing up.

"Why have you come then, Wyatt?" Uncle Ben asked. "You favor us, but somehow I don't think you just dropped in to spend the night with us and then to be off again."

"You're right, Ben. I . . . I didn't."

"What then?"

"I've come for the . . . I've come for Wes, Ben."

My heart took a leap, and I heard Aunt Mamie gasp. Uncle Ben moved closer to her, his chair squeaking on the kitchen floor. Things got so quiet I could hear the lamp flame fluttering.

"You'd take him away from us, Wyatt?" Aunt Mamie asked.

"Not if you were to say I couldn't, Sister. You've raised him. You have the right to say what happens now."

"You mean you'd go away alone if I said he should stay here with me and Ben?"

"That's what I mean. You have the right to say."

Something inside me seemed to be lurching back and forth. It was the same old battle I'd fought inside me ever since the first mention had been made of the possibility he might be coming for me. I wanted to go off to see the elephant, as the saying goes. I wanted to see and be a part of the excitement that always seemed to follow Wyatt Walker, and yet I knew I'd never leave if Aunt Mamie said I shouldn't.

"Where would you take him, Wyatt?" she asked.

"It would have to be a place away from people, some place I'm not known, or he'd be put in the danger I just spoke of. That means a place where there are few if any people at all."

"And have you thought of such a place?" Uncle Ben asked.

"I have."

"Where would that be?"

"The San Juan Mountains in southern Colorado," he said.

"What would you do there, Wyatt? What would he do?" Uncle Ben asked.

"I . . . I have a map that shows the way to a gold strike, or so the man who gave it to me claimed, and he was dying when he said it. Maybe there is gold, and maybe there isn't. If there is gold, we could come back with a stake in life for Wes. If there isn't, it won't make any difference to me. The two of us would spend the winter there together. There are things I could teach him.''

''What kind of things, Wyatt?'' Aunt Mamie asked, her voice sounding a little fearful, and there was little doubt she was thinking of the way Wyatt Walker was supposed to be able to shoot.

''Lots of things, Mamie. I could teach him to take care of himself in the wild. He could learn to track and hunt. I'd have to teach him to shoot a rifle, though. The six-gun too. But he would have to learn to be responsible with guns. We'd build ourselves a cabin for the winter. We'd put up our own food for the most part.

''Those are the kinds of thing I'd like to teach him. Maybe you don't think a man needs to know such things the way the West is becoming, but they're still good skills to have, unless the boy . . . unless Wes wants to spend his life in towns. Not that there is anything wrong with that. You only have to look at Ben if any proof at all is needed.''

He stopped talking then, and the room got even quieter. I heard a mouse's feet tinkle across a rafter above our heads. I don't think anyone else heard it, though. Their minds were too much on what had just been said and maybe about what was going to be said. I was thinking of gold and wondering why a man would give a map to its location to someone else.

''You said the man who gave you the map was dying, Wyatt. Was he a good friend of yours?'' Aunt Mamie asked.

''He turned out to be a friend.''

''Why was he dying?''

"He had consumption. I just happened to be in Santa Fe when Abe—that was his name, Abe Scott—came down from the mountains. He was already mighty sick, and he bought a house there and made the mistake of paying for it in nuggets.

"When word of his gold got around, people began to pester him to tell them where he got it. He refused, of course. Then one night some masked men broke in on him and beat him up. They said they'd kill him if he didn't talk. He wouldn't, and I guess those rowdies decided that if they killed him they would never get what they were seeking. They left, saying they'd be back.

"Abe hired me to be his bodyguard. I had never done anything like that before ... hired out my gun, you know. But somehow this seemed different. I didn't know when I took the job that Abe was dying. But in three months he was gone."

"And you took care of him," Aunt Mamie said.

"There was no one else, and he was paying me well. Before he died he gave me the map."

We sat there around the table with the lamp fluttering in our faces and thought about that story. I heard the tiny scratching of mouse feet again. Aunt Mamie looked up at the rafter the mouse was running across.

"You must do something about them, Ben," she said.

"I will, wife, but we have something more important to talk about now." Uncle Ben looked at Wyatt. "Maybe we should ask Wes what he thinks about leaving here with you, Wyatt. He's thirteen and old enough to have an opinion on what he wants to do."

"Plenty old enough," Wyatt Walker said, "and I will surely understand if he says he doesn't want to go anywhere with me."

Every eye turned to me. I swallowed hard, embarrassed that the three of them could hear it. God help me, I wanted to go, but there was all that love in Aunt Mamie's eyes, so full of it they were moist.

"I reckon I oughta stay here in Abilene," I said.

"No," Aunt Mamie said quietly. "No, you won't stay, Wes. You'll go with your father to the mountains unless you absolutely refuse. It's time the two of you got to know each other, and Wyatt's plan seems a good one. I want your word, Wyatt. I have to have it. You won't let anything happen to him. You'll bring him back safely to me, or send him back. Will you give me your word on that?"

"My word, Sister, or my life in the doing of it."

And that's the way it was decided, not by me and not by Wyatt Walker, but by Aunt Mamie, and I didn't understand then that it was because she had so much love in her heart for me, enough love to give me up.

"Will you go then, Wes?" Uncle Ben asked.

"I'll go."

And from the table across from me came a sigh from Wyatt Walker that seemed to suggest that a very heavy load had been lifted from him. And then I was angry again, for it seemed to me that the penalty for being eleven years gone should have been a heavier one.

Chapter Four

Lamplight fell through the open doorway when we rode out next morning, outlining the silhouettes of Aunt Mamie and Uncle Ben. I couldn't see their faces, but I had been given a preview at breakfast. They looked as though they thought they might never see me again. Their faces made me sad, but the excitement of riding my own horse the length of Kansas and into the mountains of Colorado took precedent. After all, it was Wyatt Walker, the famous gunslinger and gambler, I would be traveling with. Few boys, I told myself, had ever had such a chance, and the thrill of it had my heart pumping hard and fast.

We skirted Abilene to the south and then took a course west by southwest that, according to Wyatt, would take us south of Salina on the Smoky Hill River. I doubted the need for such caution that kept us from riding through town, but maybe I was hoping there might be someone awake at that hour, someone who would pass the word that they had seen Wes Walker ride out in such company. But caution was something I would get used to. Caution was second nature to Wyatt Walker. I guess you learn that when you have a killer like Lafe Kennedy on your trail.

When the sun came up, I had some of the feelings that must have afflicted old-timers when they headed west in the earlier years. Of course, there were few Indians in Kansas to be feared now, maybe an occasional party that escaped off the reservations to the south. Sometimes they came all the way to Kansas and did a little damage, maybe butchering somebody's cow or cutting a fence. When they were caught, they were taken back to the reservations. Gone too were the vast herds of buffalo that had sometimes blocked travel for days.

The terrain consisted of those rolling plains so familiar to any Kansas traveler, terrain I knew very well from having ridden it a few times with Uncle Ben when he went out to hunt. Still, it seemed different that morning, maybe because it was the first leg of a journey that was to take me to the far mountains and gold. The San Juans! The words turned into a song in my head as we rode.

I have mentioned Wyatt's caution. I saw more and more of it after the sun came up. Often he pulled up to study the horizon, paying particular attention to our back trail. I found myself wondering how a man could go through life like that, always concerned that somebody would suddenly appear and try to kill him. There couldn't be much pleasure in such a life. I saw that much from the look on his face and in his eyes as he looked for signs of pursuit.

At one stop I settled the claybank alongside and asked, "What are you looking for? Are you thinking Lafe Kennedy will come up on us?"

He thought for a moment. Then he said, "I don't know. It could be Kennedy. It could be someone else, someone who means us no harm till they see who it is. A man like myself has to know if he's going to have company.

"But the world is full of people who are out to make

mischief for others. Most of them gravitate to places where there is no law, or where the law is loose. The law eventually catches up, but till it does it's each man for himself. You're not used to that in a place like Abilene, though I remember when it was different. But there are still such places around.

"Out there in Colorado there will be some law, but it will be the loose kind, and it may be under some powerful man's thumb to be used by him as he sees fit. In that case, we'll have to look to our ownselves for our safety.

"Up there in the mountains there won't be any law at all. It'll all be up to us if anyone comes around—not that I'm expecting trouble up there."

That was a long speech, and Wyatt Walker hadn't seemed given over to that much talk before. He was giving me a different picture of where we were going too. I found myself wondering what Aunt Mamie would have said if he had talked like that before her.

"Maybe you should start teaching me to shoot if Colorado is going to be like that," I said.

He gave me a grave look, and there followed a moment of silence. "Why?" he asked. "Why do you want to learn to handle a gun?"

"Seems like a good idea if Colorado is the way you say."

"How do you feel about my being a gunfighter, Wes? Do you admire me for it?"

I had mixed feelings about it. On the one hand, I held the same view as Aunt Mamie. On the other, as I listened to all those stories of gunfights, I had to admit I found it exciting, found myself daydreaming about being a big gunfighter myself. That was something I didn't want to say right out, though, because it was right opposite to what Aunt Mamie would have wanted me to say.

"Guess I don't know how I feel," I said.

"I don't know when I'll start teaching you to shoot," he said, "or if I will. I'll have to think on it and let you know."

We rode on.

The claybank horse was a source of pride from the beginning. We traveled at that trot-canter pace which eats up the miles and still leaves a horse with something left, something Wyatt cautioned me about. The black broke a sweat before the claybank, and that was a source of pride to me as well. There were even times I had to hold him back to keep the pace Wyatt set.

I felt comfortable from the beginning at the way the claybank handled and the way he rode, easy with a swaying motion that somehow reminded me of the rolling plains that stretched out on all sides of us.

We put close to twenty miles behind us that morning before we pulled up beside the Smoky Hill River early in the afternoon.

"We'll open that bundle your Aunt Mamie packed for us," Wyatt said, stepping down.

We were still to the southeast of Salina, but my seat felt like I might have ridden there and back. I slid from the saddle and was happy to have my feet on the ground. My tailbone seemed asleep, and the insides of my legs felt raw. I figured I had learned the reason for the bowed legs of cowboys.

We loosened the cinches and watered the horses, and put them on some grass. Then we opened up Aunt Mamie's package, which held the rest of the fried chicken from the night before and some extra biscuits from breakfast. We ate our fill with our backs to the trunks of two cottonwood trees.

We didn't talk much as we ate, and when we were finished, Wyatt remained where he was. He tilted his head back against the tree and closed his eyes. I sat there and watched him and tried to figure out just how I felt about this man who had ridden into my life after eleven years. But it was something I couldn't seem to fit into words. Finally, I pushed myself up and walked beneath the trees along the stream.

A few squirrels scrambled through the branches, disturbed by my presence. A flock of birds rose in flight, their flapping wings and their chatter breaking the silence. I looked back at Wyatt. He was standing now, his six-gun drawn.

I guess the noise of the birds had woke him and made him think trouble might be at hand. He didn't say anything to me, though. He just went to the horses and began to tighten their cinches. I wasn't quite ready to ride because of the inside of my thighs, but I didn't seem to have a choice.

The afternoon wore on much as the morning with Wyatt pulling up from time to time to study the distances. A little before sundown we connected with the Solomon River. Running toward the southeast, as most water in Kansas seems to do, it wasn't much of a river at the time. But anyone who has spent time in Kansas knows what a sudden cloudburst can do. Even small streams become torrents that can devour the countryside as it sweeps everything before it. A man learns to respect even small streams in Kansas.

"We'll camp here for the night," Wyatt said. "You

see to the horses and bring in some firewood. I'll be back in a little while.''

"Where you going?'' I asked nervously.

"I'll scout around and try to shoot us a turkey for supper. These trees here look like a good place for a roost. I'll be back soon.''

He didn't reach for his rifle, and that got me curious. "You gonna shoot him down with your six-gun?'' I asked.

"Reckon I'll try.''

I'd heard of men trying to bring down a wild turkey with a six-gun. No one I knew had succeeded. A wild turkey seldom sets still long enough to be shot with any gun. They're a canny fowl. They sense a hunter's presence long before the hunter knows the bird is about. On the wing, even with a scattergun, they're hard to bring down.

He disappeared along the river, and I stripped the horses. I rubbed them down with grass and picketed them. Next I set about bringing in firewood. When I had as much as I thought we would burn I lit a small fire. Maybe thirty minutes passed before I heard the shot, a single explosion. When he strolled into camp, he carried the carcass by the feet. The turkey had already been skinned and gutted.

He rubbed some salt onto the turkey. Then he put two forked stakes into the ground across the fire from each other, fashioned a smaller, green rod, worked it through the carcass, and set the ends of it in the forks.

"Best we get ourselves a bath while this cooks,'' he said. "If we don't do it now, it might be too dark for us to see the snakes.'' The last he added almost casually.

I wasn't too much for baths in the first place, and I surely didn't cotton to taking one with snakes.

"Maybe we could take ourselves a bath in the morning in the daylight," I said.

He laughed, the first laugh I'd heard from him, and laughter on his face wrought quite a change. The years seemed to slip away in the same way they had when he stood with his arms about Aunt Mamie.

"We'll find us a place with a sandy bottom. I'll go in first and scare them off. I've been told I'm too ornery for a snake to bite."

He was as good as his word. The spot he stepped into was sandy, and the water was clear enough for the light from the waning sun to reach through to the sand. We sat in knee-deep water and soaped down, the water and soap stinging my chafed thighs and crotch. He scrubbed my back and I scrubbed his. I recall wondering what my friends back in Abilene would say if they could see me washing the back of the infamous Wyatt Walker. Maybe even Josh Hatton would realize it would be wise for him to leave me alone. Of course, he didn't seem like a gunfighter sitting there naked in the water with soap all over his back, though the Colt lay within easy reach on the bank.

I couldn't help but notice his body. He wasn't muscular. He was even a little stringy, but there was a feel and look of strength. And I counted the scars, two in his back and three in his chest. Bullet scars? I was afraid to ask.

We ate as much of the turkey as we could, washing it down with black coffee. Texas coffee, Wyatt called it. Then we sat about the fire and had a last cup. Oh, it felt fine sitting there like that, the fire crackling, and the wind whispering through the leaves overhead. For the first time in my life I felt like a man, like I was ready to face the world.

And there was comfort in the scene. That oval of fire-light was all the light there was in the world and everything beyond it was banished.

"How do you feel after your first day on the trail?" Wyatt asked.

He no longer wore the rolled-up Stetson, and his black hair fell over his ears. The soft hues of the firelight didn't show the wrinkles in his face, softening his features. As the fire blinked back at me from his eyes, I thought I was looking into the face in Aunt Mamie's picture, not the man who went crazy when Sue Ellen died.

"I feel a little raw between my legs," I said.

He was sitting with his saddle as a backrest. Reaching for his saddlebags, he rummaged through one and took out a small, round tin. Tossing it to me, he said, "Drop your pants and underwear and rub some of that in. It'll help to heal and it'll also help to toughen the skin, though the only cure is to ride till you get some saddle corns."

"Saddle corns?"

"Well, not exactly, but the skin becomes tough. I've had skin so tough between my legs from long riding I could put a needle through it without feeling any pain . . . a little like stitching leather."

I stepped from the light and dropped my pants. When I applied the salve, the cool coating seemed to help.

When I came back in, the fire had begun to die a little. I sat down. After a moment I said, "Tell me about the gold."

"Ah, the gold. Are you excited about going to the mountains to look for gold?"

"I've not seen mountains, and I'm excited about that," I said. "As for the gold, I'm not against finding some."

That wasn't how I felt. In fact, there was that twinge of excitement whenever I thought of it. I wasn't sure I wanted Wyatt Walker to know of that feeling, though.

"You don't seem to be too stirred up over it," he said.

"I'm not."

"That'll change as you get older if you turn out to be like other men."

"Could I see the map?"

He reached for his saddlebags, searched through them, and brought out a piece of paper, which he handed over to me. I spread it out. It showed a single, wavy line that curled through other lines that were marked as mountains. The darker line was marked with X's and each had its own inscription such as "granite-faced bluff," or "rabbit ears peak." The final X had the inscription "lonesome pine" written beside it. Lonesome pine. It sounded a little ominous.

The paper was almost worn through its creases, as though it had been carried in someone's pocket or saddlebag for a very long time. There were dark splotches on the surface that looked like rusty water had dripped on it. It crinkled in my hands as I folded it up and passed it back across the fire.

"Do you think there'll be gold there?" I asked.

"Not really."

"Then why are we going to look for it?"

"I spoke the truth last night," he said. "If there is gold, well and good. It'll be yours, and you'll be free to do with it what you will. But if there isn't, well, that'll be all right too. We'll hunt and fish together. We'll build us a winter cabin and cure our own meat. It'll be just the two of us with no one else around. We'll be up high where the air is clean and fresh. . . ."

His voice sort of drifted off as if he was seeing too strongly what he had been speaking of and couldn't waste the time to describe the vision to me, like he had to just sit there and enjoy it in silence. It was a little like Aunt Mamie and the Reverend Todd Baker sounded when they spoke of heaven.

I have to believe Wyatt had fashioned a dream for himself during those years of wandering, a dream that involved the two of us living away from the world. That was what he saw as he stared into the darkness beyond the fire.

I've often wondered if partly I wasn't a substitute for Sue Ellen. Maybe I'm wrong. Maybe he had me and only me in mind. I'd like to think that was true. But I must have felt a little like the substitute that night, or I probably wouldn't have put my next question to him so bluntly.

"Why did you just leave me and turn to gambling and the gun when she died?" I asked.

I thought I saw him shudder. The fire had continued to die down, so I may be mistaken. At any rate, he didn't answer for a time. He even closed his eyes, as if he knew they might let whatever he was feeling inside leak out.

I waited nervously.

"I can't answer that," he said finally. "I doubt I'll ever be able to answer it. What I do know is that the world changed for me that day, changed into something I couldn't seem to face. The very thought that time could pass without her in the world was a torment.

"I think I felt like I had to dish out some punishment to a world which had somehow taken her away. That idea stayed with me for years. Then I began to feel sick inside about something else. This time it was what I had become. I wanted to change, but I was in too deep. Wading out of a slough is never easy, and you never come out clean.

"Then came that night in El Paso. Suddenly, in the very middle of it, as I drew down on a man whose first name I didn't even know, I thought of you, boy, and her too, and she seemed to reach out from her grave and scold me.

"I saw you as you were when I handed you over into Mamie's arms, and I recalled how Mamie looked standing there holding the bundle in that blanket, with Ben standing behind her, both of them looking sad enough to end it all.

"I killed that man that night. Then I killed his brother. I did it so I could stay alive, but as I killed I made myself the promise I would come back to Abilene, that I'd try to somehow make it up to you.

"But that wasn't all. I wanted to see what you'd become. I wanted to know how much of her was in you. And last, and most important, I wanted to see if I could become a father."

"It took you a long time to make Abilene," I said. "That fight was over a year ago."

I can't describe what I was feeling. I know I felt anger and hurt, and my throat seemed almost closed off. I was glad it was dark, because I could feel tears in my eyes as well.

"I know," he said. "I know it was a long time. But Lafe Kennedy was after me. I didn't want to bring my trouble down on you and Ben and Mamie. If I had it to do over again I would go into the street and finish him off.''

"Why didn't you?" I asked.

"It seemed like I couldn't do any more killing with the picture of you and Sue Ellen before my eyes. Now I wish I had. Lafe Kennedy doesn't deserve to live after all the killing and robbing he's done. Maybe I don't deserve to live, either, for I've done my share of killing, but I can say truthfully I never shot a man except in defense of my own life.

"Maybe that's no excuse, but it's the truth. And if I'd killed the last Kennedy that night, maybe I wouldn't have to be slipping off to the mountains just to spend some time with my son.''

I don't think he was talking to me so much as he was talking to himself. It's possible he had even forgotten for the moment I was there.

The fire was nothing more than a few red coals now, and its dim red light turned his face to shades of red and flickered a few dim shadows back and forth across it as he talked. The crickets chirped, the horses pulled at the grass, and occasionally a coal snapped and spread some sparks around.

I felt the need to say something, but my mind seemed to have lost any power to work. I reckon I was too full of feelings for talk.

Finally, he pushed himself up and spread his bedroll. "You should do the same," he said to me. "Morning will come before you know it, and we will put in fifty miles tomorrow." He seemed to have tucked the turmoil away inside him somewhere.

"I shouldn't bring things like that up," I said.

"No, you have the right. Sores have to bleed their pus out before they can heal. I'm speaking for both of us when I say there is sometimes a responsibility for people to say whatever it is they feel. Now is such a time for us, and I hope you won't hold back when there is something on your mind."

He slipped his boots off and crawled between his blankets. Before he stretched out he placed the holstered Colt near his head where his hand would barely have to reach out to get to it. Next he carefully put the turned-up Stetson over the gun, maybe to keep the dew from it, I decided.

I turned in myself shortly afterward to the song of the crickets and locusts and the sound of the wind moving the leaves overhead. The fire was out, but the moon had risen; its light fell through the branches and dappled the ground around me. Beyond the moon, the stars seemed very high, and I thought they were brighter than I had ever seen before.

A coyote called from the distance. A mate answered, in a barking way that then fell off into a wail. I had heard that song many times before, but there was something different about it that night, something sadder and sweeter, and yet tinged with danger too.

Chapter Five

Despite the nagging fear brought on by Wyatt's constant attention to our back trail, I enjoyed those first few days. They were days in which the claybank cemented a place in my heart.

Wyatt was pleased at the way the horse and I took to each other. Though he never spoke of it, I could see it in his eyes as he watched us. Once he told me he thought I might turn out to have a way with horses, a gift some people were born with, he said.

But my growing attachment to the claybank, and his to me, wasn't the only thing I enjoyed. I found I liked being with Wyatt too. He had a way of showing me how to do things—make coffee, tie a knot, trail a deer. He was always patient, but he could reprimand, like once when I was holding the rifle wrong, the barrel pointing directly at my foot.

Coming to me, he took the rifle roughly from me and said, "Hold a long gun like this, away from anything you don't intend to shoot at. Then, if it goes off accidentally, you won't shoot something you didn't intend to." He gave a demonstration of what he meant, and there was in his manner something harsh but special in the way he did it—a regard for me, I knew.

I was surprised after a few days to find I wasn't seeing or thinking of him as the famous gunslinger. I guess I was beginning to see him all the time like I had that night when we sat naked together in the Solomon River, though I still couldn't find it in me to call him "Pa."

Nor was it just Wyatt and the claybank I took pleasure from. We took our time crossing Kansas, hunted and fished when there was opportunity, and many times went into camp early where we sat around the fire and talked.

Wyatt invited questions, not with words so much as in his manner. Though I stayed away from the personal stuff, there were other things to talk about, like some of the places he'd been and the people he'd met.

During such talks, I think I found out why Aunt Mamie loved him so much, and why she didn't want to talk about the ugly things he did after Sue Ellen was killed.

Then I found out he had known Wild Bill Hickok!

Wild Bill was a special hero of mine, partly because he had once served as marshal in Abilene. But it was more than that. He had the reputation of being a straight shooter, and I don't mean with a gun, though he was plenty good with those.

While he was in Abilene he got into a gunfight with Phil Coe over a picture Coe and his partner hung over the entrance to the Bull's Head Saloon, a picture that showed the parts of a bull that nice people seemed not to want to see.

Wild Bill asked Coe to take it down. Coe refused, so Wild Bill took it down himself. That was the start of the trouble between them that finally led to the gunplay in which Coe was killed.

Wild Bill went on the stage for a while in Buffalo Bill Cody's Wild West Show. He also had an outstanding record as a scout for the Army.

"I knew him in Deadwood," Wyatt said to me one

night, when I mentioned how I felt about Wild Bill. "He showed up there to prospect, but he didn't work at taking out any gold."

"What did he do?" I asked.

"Mostly he gambled."

"Did you ever have a game with him?"

"A few."

"Who won?"

"First one, then the other."

"Were you there when 'Broken Nosed Jack' McCall shot him in the back?"

"I was."

"Tell me about it?"

"It was in the No. Ten Saloon. McCall just walked up behind him and shot him. Hickok was holding a hand of aces over eights. Those cards have ever since been known as the dead man's hand.

"I've known men to get up and leave a game when they drew that hand, even though they might have won the pot. I guess they remembered what happened to Hickok, and they didn't want to take any chances."

I already knew what happened to McCall. He beat the murder charge at his trial in Deadwood, but he was later arrested in Cheyenne and sent to the federal court in Yankton where he was convicted and hanged. A lot of folks traveled there to see him swing.

But back to Wyatt. How could you not respect a man who had played poker with Wild Bill?

We spotted the plume of dust early one morning. Wyatt's face tightened considerably as we sat and studied it.

"Are they trailing us?" I asked.

"They could be. We'll watch awhile and see."

"What'll we do if they are?"

"We'll think on that."

"How many?" I asked.

"Maybe half a dozen."

I felt a little jolt of coldness. A half dozen men back there who might be on our trail! I could see them loaded down with guns and riding hard.

"How far back?" I asked.

"I'd say about ten miles."

Then I asked the question that was really in my mind. "Is it Lafe Kennedy, do you think?"

"Let's don't anticipate trouble till it comes down on us," Wyatt said.

We didn't try to outdistance them, and we didn't try to cover our sign. I didn't have to ask why. Wyatt intended to see if it was us they were after by leaving it clear. We zigzagged from time to time, once riding toward a particularly tall cottonwood. We stopped briefly at the stream that ran beneath the tree and watered the horses and ourselves. A few miles later we topped out on the crest of a bluff and turned back to watch.

"We'll see if they take that north turn and go to the tree," Wyatt said. "If they do, we'll have our answer."

We sat there maybe forty-five minutes. Most of the time the tail of dust remained constant. Once it disappeared, and I thought the riders had stopped. I drew a breath of relief, but found it premature, for when the dust rose up again, it was headed directly for that big tree. They stopped there to water their horses too. There could be no doubt they were following us.

I suddenly heard myself breathing a little harder, and my hands turned sweaty. A drop of sweat as cold as an icicle trailed down my side.

"Well, we have the answer, don't we?" Wyatt said. It was a question, but it didn't call for an answer.

"It's Lafe Kennedy, isn't it?" I said.

"Probably."

"How could he have got on our trail?"

"I expect he found out where I was heading when I left Texas. He may have sent someone ahead on the train to look out for me. After that all he had to do was cut our sign south of town."

"How would he know it was us?"

"He's followed me before. He'd know the black's print."

"What're we gonna do?"

"Stay ahead the rest of the day, and maybe even let them gain a little."

"Let them gain?"

"Until tonight," he said.

"Who do you suppose are the men with Kennedy?"

"I have reason to know them well enough. They were in on that ambush down in Texas. There is Big John Bodie who rode for a time with Jesse and Frank James. He's been on the outside of the law ever since. And there is Frank Stoudamire. He killed a neighbor and his family back in Louisiana in a dispute over some land. I guess he found a taste of killing. He's been doing it ever since.

"Jack 'Broken Jaw' Johnson is a rowdy who worked on the docks in Galveston for a while. He robbed the company, killed two clerks who recognized him, and wounded another. He fled to Mexico, joined some bandits working both sides of the Rio Grande in the Nueces Strip country. He met up with Pacheco Padilla down there. The two have been together ever since. Padilla was one of Juan Cortina's lieutenants for a while."

"Who was Juan Cortina?" I asked.

"A Mexican general who ruled the country around Matamoros for years. He and much of his army made a living from stealing Texas cattle and horses and running them back over the border where they were shipped to Cuba. The Texas Rangers have been after Padilla and Johnson ever since they cleaned up the Nueces area, but they've never been able to catch up to them."

"How did Johnson get the nickname 'Broken Jaw'?" I asked.

"He got into a fight in Matamoros. The fella he was fighting with hit him across the face with a singletree and broke his jawbone. The bones were so smashed the doctor had to take some out. It twisted his mouth about. For a long time he didn't eat anything that wasn't liquid. Then he found he could poke something solid into his mouth with his fingers. At least that's the story I heard."

"You said there were probably six back there. Counting Lafe Kennedy that makes five," I said.

"The last is an outlaw named Rudabaugh Reese. Men wonder about him. He's young, well educated, and handsome. He is said to be the son of a wealthy man in Philadelphia."

"How could he go wrong then?" I asked.

"What makes one horse a renegade, another content to be broke and rode? I don't know the answer. Maybe something happened back there in Philadelphia that caused him to go bad. Maybe he just naturally is. I heard that a sister once came west and hunted till she found him. She tried to talk him into returning home with her.

"I never had a run in with Reese, but he might be the most dangerous of the lot, because you don't expect a man like that to be a killer."

I had heard a lot about Rudabaugh Reese. There was a story of a gunfight he'd been in down in Presidio, the little town on the Rio Grande. It was said that he outdrew and shot two men, that neither of them had managed to draw their guns. There were stories too of what a ladies' man he was, and how he could talk himself out of any jam. In fact, he had been compared to Wyatt from time to time.

We sat there a moment longer studying the rooster tail of dust, and I thought of the names Wyatt had just ticked off. Most of them I'd heard of, but then they were the names of distant badmen. Now they were the names of men who were chasing me, and the thought of falling into the hands of any one of them sent shivers up my spine.

"Well, we better get under way," Wyatt said.

I took a final look at the rising dust and fell in behind him.

The only stops we made for the rest of that day were to water and rest the horses, and we didn't ride too hard. We did it like the cavalry does—fifty minutes of riding and ten minutes of rest.

Wyatt produced some jerky from his saddlebag and we chewed that as we rode, washing it down with water from our canteens.

"What is it you plan for us to do tonight?" I finally asked.

"We'll double back, and I'll slip into their camp and chase their horses off. We'll put some miles between us and them while they're on foot, miles they won't be able to make up unless they're riding some mighty good horseflesh."

"What'll I be doing while you're scattering their horses?"

"You'll be staying with ours."

At sundown we rode into a bunch of trees, a circle of oaks, cottonwood, and willow. And I remembered what Uncle Ben had once told me. He said that in Kansas you know there is water around when you see trees. "It may be just beneath the ground, but most of the time it's on the surface." We found the small spring in among the trees.

We stripped the horses, rubbed them down, and picketed them on some good grass near the spring. Saying it was best we didn't light a fire to cook, Wyatt opened a tin of crackers and a can of beans, which we split between us. We ate from the same can of beans, passing it back and forth.

"We'll stretch out and rest a couple of hours," he said when we were finished.

Using his saddle for a pillow, he was soon breathing regularly. I couldn't sleep. I kept thinking of that gang of badmen back there. Their names sounded like a roll call of the worst of western outlaws, and lying there in the dark, I began to make up faces for the names. The worst-looking of the lot was Broken Jaw Johnson. I pictured him hunched over a plate as he poked food into his mouth. As he ate, his beady dark eyes kept circling, trying to find someone who watched him with anything but respect.

And there was Lafe Kennedy, the man who had sworn to kill Wyatt and had already tried to do it once. I didn't have to imagine what he looked like. I had seen a picture of him in the paper. Then I started to think of what was going to happen if we did fall into their hands. For sure they'd kill Wyatt, but what about me? Of course, they would know I was Wyatt's son, and they surely wouldn't just turn me loose. No, they'd probably kill me first with Wyatt looking on just to dish out more punishment to him.

I thought about Aunt Mamie and Uncle Ben. They might still be sitting at the supper table. Uncle Ben would be telling Aunt Mamie anything interesting that happened at the store. Aunt Mamie would listen quietly, commenting on whatever it was when Uncle Ben was finished. I wondered if they would speak of me, and if they might have some inkling of what might be about to happen. There had been times when Aunt Mamie had seemed to know it beforehand when something bad was in store. Would she be having one of those premonitions about now?

Finally, I dozed off.

Wyatt's hand on my shoulder brought me awake.

"It's time," he said.

I was surprised by the sliver of light on his face, for we hadn't built a fire before for obvious reasons. This fire was small and burned from inside a hole maybe a foot deep, casting its light only upward.

"It's the way Comanches build a fire at night," he explained when he saw my surprise. "If you don't stand above it, it's hard to spot from any distance."

Both horses were already saddled, but Wyatt had made coffee, and we squatted on our heels back from the fire and drank a cup.

There wasn't a smidgen of wind blowing through the trees. Maybe it was because we were there, but the frogs that usually gather at a spring were silent, and the crickets too.

"I shouldn't have brought you away from Abilene," Wyatt said, breaking the silence. "Maybe I shouldn't ever have come there. I'm beginning to think my promise to bring you back safe to Mamie was rash."

I didn't have to ask him why. There was that gang back there, and now we took it for granted who they were, just as we took for granted what they would do if they caught us.

"Are you sorry you did?" I asked.

"Sorry only for one thing—that I have put you in danger. As for the rest, no, I'm not sorry. It's something I should have done long ago. I'm most sorry I didn't do it before I had to kill those Kennedys. Naturally, I thought I'd given Lafe Kennedy the slip, that we'd be able to get out of Kansas and bury ourselves in the San Juans till he lost his killing urge. There is a choice for you, though, Wes."

"What?"

"You can ride to the south and then circle back when you're well beyond where they are. You won't have to avoid the towns on the ride back. You can hit one, buy a railroad ticket for yourself and passage for the clay-bank. I'll give you the money. You can be back in Abilene in three days at the most."

"No."

"No what?"

"No, I won't leave you."

I hadn't planned to say it. I hadn't *planned* to say anything at all. It just came out. Afterward I knew why it did. I hadn't admitted it, but he had come more and more to feel like my pa. During those few days as we rode across Kansas, something had happened between us. Those feelings that had kept Wyatt away from me had been slowly swept aside, and my resentment that he had stayed away so long was gone as well.

"You're sure of that?" he asked, and I could hear a quality in his voice that I put down as relief no matter how guarded it sounded.

"I'm sure.

"I reckon I oughta order you to go, but somehow I can't seem to bring myself to do it, and why you'd show loyalty to me, I don't know. But I thank you. I just hope I never have to face Mamie and explain why I'm letting you do it."

"You won't ever have to tell her. We'll get out of this."

"How come you're so sure?"

"Since I can remember I've been hearing stories about you getting out of tight scrapes. No man ever outthought you. No man ever outdrew you. You're Wyatt Walker. I reckon that's why I'm sure."

"A lot of that stuff was made up," he said. "And I have to tell you I don't feel like the fella in those stories. I doubt if I ever did. What I wish now is that there had never been a grain of truth in them, that they had never got started. Then I reckon things would be different with us."

He got up and dumped the rest of the coffee over the fire. Then he took our cups and the coffeepot and put them in the pack.

"We better ride," he said.

The night was very dark. What light there was—and it didn't amount to much—trickled down from distant stars. I put the claybank on the black's tail and gave him loose rein. He stayed there, and most of the time I could see no farther than his ears.

From time to time Wyatt pulled up to study the darkness and sniff the air.

"If you smell smoke, let me know," he told me once, his voice low in the darkness but carrying strong.

Seemed to me we rode for hours, but it couldn't have been more than about three. Clouds drifted out of the northwest and hid the stars. The only sounds were the creak of leather, a muffled sound from a hoof, or one of the horses suddenly blowing out a nostril. Then Wyatt pulled up, and the claybank stopped with his nose almost touching the black's rear.

"What is it?" I asked.

"We should have seen their fire by now," he said. "I'm beginning to think we bypassed them in the dark."

"But they would have had a fire, wouldn't they?"

"If they didn't get drunk and let it go out."

We sat there a few minutes in darkness that was almost complete. The black horse suddenly shook his head and stamped a couple of times.

"He smells something," Wyatt said. "We'll top the next rise and see what's below."

We moved out, and though I couldn't see anything I could tell we were soon climbing from the way I had to hold to the saddlehorn. When we reached the crest, Wyatt pulled up, and below maybe a mile away a fire winked back up at us.

"It's them," Wyatt said, swinging down. "We'll walk from here."

We started down, Wyatt in the lead, of course, and went slow enough to feel for our footing. We stopped out from the fire, and we were still looking down on it. There was a bush nearby, and we tied the horses off.

"Just in case they get a little nervous when the shooting starts."

"Shooting?" I asked.

"I'm going down there and cut their horses loose. I'll
fire a shot to stampede them. When you hear that shot,
you pour some lead into their camp."

He gave me his rifle when he said that.

"You mean I should try to kill them?" I asked.

"You can try if you have a mind to, but I don't think
you can this far off. But it'll scare them, make them
hunker down so I can get away."

I could see the men about the fire clearly enough to
count them—six, as Wyatt had said there would be. They
looked like mighty big men, and their faces were
bearded. I tried to put names to them as I had done in
my thoughts, but I had no way of knowing if I got any
of them right. I was too far away even to see Broken
Jaw Johnson's mouth. As they sat around the fire, a bottle passed among them.

"Which one is Lafe Kennedy?" I asked.

"See the big one? He's directly across the fire and
facing us."

"I see him."

"That's Kennedy."

I still couldn't make out his features, but he looked as
big as a grizzly sitting there and taking a pull from the
bottle when it reached him. Somebody must have told a
joke, for there was a burst of laughter. It rose up out of
the shallow valley and echoed hollowly a couple of
times.

"I'm going now," Wyatt said. "Will you be all
right?"

I told him yes, but I felt anything but confident. He

disappeared into the night, and I was left there with only the horses to keep me company and the view of the drunken outlaws below.

I crouched down, the rifle in my hands, and took a couple of practice aims at the campfire. I decided I'd try to shoot into the fire and scatter it. Then I felt the rifle slip in my hands and became aware of how damp my palms were. I wiped them on my britches and kept doing that.

Their horses were on a picket line maybe fifty yards from the fire. I couldn't see a guard on them, but the light from the fire didn't reach out there very well. I kept my eyes there, hoping to know when Wyatt moved in. Then I saw him, and the horses began to stir as he turned them loose. He disappeared into the darkness, and I waited for the sound of his six-gun. It came, and I jumped despite my anticipation.

The horses began to scatter in all directions. The men about the fire were suddenly running like stirred-up ants, and they began blasting away in the direction Wyatt had fired from. I wondered if one of them had caught a glimpse of him, or if they were just firing back at the sound of his gun, for I could hear his answering blasts from out there in the darkness and see the momentary flash from his gun.

I lifted the rifle, took aim at the fire, and squeezed off a shot. I don't know where the bullet went, but it must have come close. The men, already lying flat, began to scratch and claw their way off into the darkness. I kept on pumping and firing. I don't know how much time passed. It seemed like none at all before Wyatt was beside me.

He took the rifle from my hands, saying, "You did well. Now let's ride out of here."

We didn't push the horses too hard. I was feeling good from the praise, and I wasn't sweating anymore. I sent the claybank along beside the black, riding even with Wyatt.

"How far will their horses run?" I asked.

"If I had my way they'd run all the way to Texas, but they won't. They'll stop after a few miles and begin to graze. Some may even wander back into camp come morning, but they'll be held up a day, maybe more, while they round up the others. Hopefully, it'll give us the time we need."

At the crest of the slope we stopped and looked back into the valley. There was no fire down there now and no noise . . . just the dark well we were looking into.

A question had been in my mind ever since I'd asked Wyatt if he wanted me to shoot to kill. "Why didn't you just aim the rifle at Kennedy and kill him? You could have picked him off easy enough from up there on the slope."

"I never ambushed a man," he said, "and I hope to God I never stoop so low."

"But he's tried to ambush you once. He'll try again if he catches up to us."

"You may never understand it, but there are only two things that separate me from the likes of Lafe Kennedy."

I didn't say anything . . . I couldn't.

"I never stole, and I never killed a man from ambush. That may not be much to claim, but I've always hoped it set me apart from the likes of Kennedy." His voice was dark, moody, and there was silence for a moment.

Then he said, "You feel like riding all night?" and his voice was natural again.

"All day tomorrow too." I said.

He gave a little laugh, catching my meaning. I laughed too, but it sounded strained. I felt like we were partners, though, and it was a good feeling riding through the night like that. But the feeling wasn't to last long.

Chapter Six

We rode for hours that night beneath a quarter moon that gave the rolling terrain a silver look and turned the occasional thin line of trees into shadowy sentinels. I got sleepy a few times despite the danger we were running from. Wyatt did nothing to hide our trail, and I asked him why.

"Miles are more important tonight," he said.

"But why north?"

"Denver is there. Maybe they'll think that's where we're heading. There's lots of gambling. It's a logical place for Kennedy to think I might go."

I was never so tired. I had spent the day in the saddle, rested only a couple of hours, and now had been riding most of the night. But my seat and thighs had toughened. I was thankful for that.

About the time a pinkish glow appeared to the east, we topped a rise, and below us, winding along the foot of the ridge, was a line of trees. In the quickening light, I saw running water through the branches. Its soft purr reached up to us.

"The Arkansas," Wyatt said.

I had little idea where we were, though I'd certainly heard of the Arkansas River. Wyatt swung down and took a worn map from his saddlebag. Spreading it on the ground, he said, "Come down here a second, and I'll show you where you are."

I slid down and crouched beside him.

"Here," he said, locating the spot on the map with his finger. "See the horseshoe the river makes?"

"Yes."

"We're just about at its northernmost point."

"How far have we come?"

Studying the map a moment, he said, "I'd estimate four hundred miles."

"How much farther to the San Juans?"

He unrolled the map a little more. "Trinidad is here. The San Juans are to the west . . . those wavy lines. We'll cross into Colorado in a couple of days . . . right here, and cut south to Trinidad."

"You mean, we'll ride into a town?" I asked, for that was something we hadn't done since leaving Abilene.

"We have to pick up enough supplies for the winter," he explained. "Maybe I won't be recognized this far west. We'll just buy what we need and ride out again."

"How many miles to Trinidad?"

"Two hundred, maybe a little more."

He didn't seem inclined to move at once down the slope to the river. I took advantage of that and asked him to tell me about Trinidad.

"I've never been there, but I've been told it's small. It sets just north of Raton Pass, about the only way to get into New Mexico Territory from the north. The Santa Fe Trail runs through the town. There are mining camps and some outlying ranches."

We climbed back up and rode down to the Arkansas. I had heard stories about it. I had been at the train station in Abilene many times when cowboys, taking the train back to Texas, got off to stretch their legs. Following along behind them, I'd heard them speak of crossing the Arkansas at flood stage and how dangerous that was. But now the river was low, no more than fifteen feet at the widest places. We sat our mounts on its bank and looked it over.

"Old Bent's Fort is to the west of here," Wyatt said. "The Arkansas runs past it. The Bent brothers built the fort as a trading post. It helped to open up this country."

"Is it still there?" I asked.

"No, it was torn down and deserted some years ago."

We camped back from the river beneath some trees. Wyatt built a fire beneath a bushy oak. He told me to notice how the limbs and leaves scattered and thinned the smoke so it couldn't be seen from very far away.

He cooked up a good meal—a flour hoecake, some antelope and bean stew, and some coffee as black as midnight that scalded my throat as it went down.

We had already seen to the horses, and, dousing the fire with water from the creek, we unrolled our blankets for a couple of hours' sleep. I didn't think once of the hardness of the ground and went to sleep watching a black-billed magpie perched in a bush maybe twenty yards away. He was eyeing the campsite looking for something to steal.

Wyatt shook me awake sometime later. He had coffee made and the horses were saddled. We drank coffee and then climbed up. Wyatt led off, sending the black into the Arkansas, and then headed west, keeping to the river's edge. We rode in the water all that day except when we stopped to rest. When we came out, he chose a rocky spot on the bank where our tracks didn't show.

I never saw so much wildlife as there was along the

Arkansas. We scared up deer and rabbits from the rushes. Once I saw a raccoon doing his fishing in broad daylight.

About an hour before dark, we made camp in a thick grove of cottonwoods. I saw to the horses while Wyatt fished. That night we ate fried trout, fried cornbread, and wild greens. Dessert was a can of peaches, which we shared.

As tired as we were, neither of us slept well. Maybe it was because we both had thoughts of Lafe Kennedy and his gang. I heard Wyatt get up several times. Once he walked from beneath the trees, studied the night for a long while, and then came back to his blankets.

Next morning we cleared away any signs of our camp, burying the coals and pouring water over the fresh dirt. Before we took to the Arkansas, Wyatt cut himself a limb with a bushy top. When we left the river again, he tied a rope to the limb and tossed the line to me.

"Drag it along behind you to wipe out our prints," he said.

"Won't they just trail us by that?" I asked a little later, indicating the yard-wide swath scratched out from dragging the bush.

"If the wind doesn't wipe it out, or if it doesn't rain. But if we have a little of either, it'll get those brush marks. Hoofprints are harder to wipe out."

I pulled the branch along behind us till it wore down to a nub, or rather, the claybank pulled it. About the middle of the afternoon Wyatt turned the black about and pulled up behind me. Stepping down, he took the rope from the brush. Tossing the rope to me, he left the brush where it was. Later that night it rained, rained hard, and though we got soaked along with our bedding, there was the satisfaction of knowing that Lafe Kennedy would have a harder time picking up our trail.

We still hadn't talked much about the gold. I suppose it wasn't too much on either of our minds. When I did think about it, I got a little excited at what we could do if we struck it rich.

Our spirits lifted with the rain, but the easy feeling of those first few days didn't return. Lafe Kennedy had changed that. We did stop to hunt once or twice. I remember the way Wyatt tricked a small herd of antelope in close so he could shoot one. He tied a white shirt on a limb, lay in the grass, and waved the shirt aloft slowly.

The antelopes showed some curiosity and began to come toward the shirt. When the first was close enough, Wyatt eased up out of the grass and shot him. We skinned him out and roasted as much of the meat as Wyatt thought we would use before it spoiled. If Lafe Kennedy hadn't been back there, we would have taken the time to smoke the rest and pack it along.

During that leg of the ride, I became aware that something was happening to me. For instance, I found myself noticing so much more of what was around me. There was the blueness of the sky, the smells on the wind, and the way the white clouds built up and then drifted across the heavens. I began to think there was even beauty in the never-ending, treeless vistas that turned more and more to desert. I took in the condition of the grass, noted the animals, and found myself observing landmarks. But always I kept an eye toward the west and waited for the mountains to appear, my heart ticking a little faster at the thought.

Once a dark cloud formed overhead and in minutes began to pour rain down on us. A furious wind seized us, at times threatening to take me out of the saddle. Then there was a few moments of calm followed by hail. We had to dismount and crouch to the leeward side of the horses for protection. I remember the drama of the zigzag flash of lightning across the dark sky and the roll of the thunder.

"When will we be in Colorado?" I asked Wyatt a couple of days later.

We were stopped beneath a lone oak on a rise. The horses with lowered heads pulled at the sparse grass. In every direction the country seemed to roll on and on with little to distract the eye till earth and heaven met. It seemed barren and empty, but no country ever is.

"We're in Colorado now," he said.

"But where are the mountains?"

"We should be able to see them soon."

Late that afternoon we came on a shallow ravine with water. There was a small stream no wider than my hand. It meandered a few yards and disappeared into the sand.

"We better take advantage of it," Wyatt said, referring to the water. "It might be the last we find between here and Trinidad. We'll have to dig out a pool for the horses to drink, and we won't have to dig it much deeper for us to take a bath. You do the digging, and I'll set up camp and get supper cooking."

I swung down, gave him the claybank's reins, and began to scoop the sand out with my hands. Except for a rock now and then the digging was easy. I widened the stream and dug down a foot or more, the current carrying the muddy water away. By then Wyatt had set up in a pocket of the ravine, and the smell of our supper drifted back to me. I called to him, and he brought the horses down to drink.

After they were picketed, Wyatt invited me to take my bath while he finished cooking. I sat in the little pool, lathered up, and enjoyed the aroma of coffee and roasting antelope. Mixed in was the smell of curing grass and rain falling on parched earth somewhere off in the distance.

Well before the sun went down, we'd had our baths, eaten our supper, and were cleaning the cooking utensils. I saw Wyatt watching the black horse, who had lifted his head and seemed to be hearing or smelling something beyond the rim of the ravine. Both horses gave a low whicker then, and Wyatt put the utensils aside and stood up.

"Let's get back into camp," he said.

"What do you think it is?" I asked, following him.

"Maybe just some wild animal, but we won't take any chances."

He crossed to his warbag, untied it, and rummaged around in it for a moment. When his hand came out, it held a Colt six-gun that was twin to the one he wore. Handing the gun to me buttfirst, he said, "I don't expect you'll have to use it, but hold on to it while I'm gone."

"Where're you going?" I asked, not able to hide my alarm at being left there in the ravine by myself.

"Up there to have a look."

"Why don't I go with you?"

"What if it's Indians sneaking up to steal the horses?" he asked.

We had barely talked of Indians, and my heart gave a lurch. "Are you saying we're in Indian country now?" I asked.

"Have been for a day or so. Jicarilla Apaches roam through here from the south, and these used to be the hunting grounds of the Arapaho. Do you know how to use a six-gun?'' he asked.

That took my mind off Indians for the moment. ''I've shot Uncle Ben's.''

''Good! Keep it handy. During the next few days, maybe we'll do a little shooting together.''

I stood with the six-gun clasped before me as Wyatt crossed the ravine and began to climb the far side. The horses watched Wyatt as well, their ears thrown forward.

To the west the sun was only a half circle; half of the blood red ball was already swallowed up by the horizon. Something moved farther down the ravine from the horses, and I watched a half-grown coyote slink from the brush to lap rapidly from the little stream. Overhead a hawk circled in the red sun's light. I stood there with my back pressed against the rocky side of the pocket we were camped in. I held the six-gun tightly, as though it might take a notion to jump out of my hand.

''Boy, you're squeezing that gun so hard your fingers are going to sink into it,'' a voice said from just above me.

My knees went weak. I thought I might sink to the ground before I could turn around and look up, but somehow I managed. He was crouched on a ledge a few yards above me. For a moment I thought he was a wild man about to sail down from his perch in the rocks.

''Who are you? What do you want?'' I managed to ask.

''The name is Buckhorn Smith,'' he said. ''I smelled your coffee and hoped you'd invite me into camp for a cup.''

''You're not one of Lafe Kennedy's men, are you?'' I asked.

"No, but if you're Wyatt Walker's boy and that was Wyatt Walker himself I saw climbing out of the ravine over there, I bring you word of Kennedy."

"Are they out there somewhere near?"

"No, the last I saw of them was in Dodge City. They were guzzling whiskey and lamenting on their bad luck. Seems like some of them had walked a number of miles to round up their horses. They had come in to town to recuperate, as the saying goes.

"I'm coming down now," he said, "and I'd appreciate your turning that hawgleg a little more to the right, Mr. Walker."

"Wes," I said weakly as he landed before me.

"And you can call me Buckhorn." He offered me his hand, which I shook.

He wasn't much taller than I was, and as slender as a willow switch. He was dressed in buckskin, the shirt V-necked and laced with rawhide string, and there was fringe along the seams of the arms and shoulders. The buckskin pants looked a little more slick. They were fringed as well. His moccasins looked to be new.

He wore a grizzled beard, which grew out of skin as tough-looking as leather. The face was bony and criss-crossed with wrinkles. They spread out from his eyes and his mouth in a fan shape. His hair was gray and very long. He wore it tied in a ponytail that fell down his back. His brows were prominent, thick, and gray, and recessed dark eyes twinkled out at me.

I went to the fire, poured him a cup of coffee, and brought it back to him.

"Thank'ee, young Wes," he said, taking the cup and sitting on a rock I had rolled in for a chair.

"Are you all right down there, Wes?" Wyatt asked from the rim of the ravine.

I looked up at him. He was crouched down so as not to outline himself on the rim. He held the reins of a red mule whose head I could just make out.

"I'm fine, but we got company, a Mr. Buckhorn Smith," I said.

"I'd be obliged if you'd bring that ornery mule down with you when you come, Mr. Walker," Buckhorn said. "His name is Old Sinner, and if he does anything mean just give him a good kick."

"I'll bring him down," Wyatt called.

We found places about the fire and each had a cup in his hand.

I said to Wyatt, "Buckhorn here just came from Dodge. He saw Lafe Kennedy there."

"Sat next to him in the Longhorn Saloon while he and his gang of cutthroats had a drink. I never listened to a man so filled with hate, Mr. Walker."

"Call me Wyatt."

"Wyatt," Buckhorn Smith acknowledged. "He said as many as three times what he intended to do to you over that one drink."

"I thought he might give it up and head for Texas after I drove their horses off the other night," Wyatt said. "I thought it might show them just how easy it would be for me to take action against them. Are they behind you, Buckhorn?"

"A couple of days, I expect. They hadn't finished their drinking when I rode out, and they won't cover as much ground as I do. Old Sinner can outdistance most any hoss over a period of time."

He gazed at the long-eared mule fondly, and the ani-

mal lifted his head and shook it up and down a couple
of times as if to agree with Buckhorn.

"You didn't ride out here and pick up our trail just to
tell us you saw Kennedy, did you, Buckhorn?" Wyatt
asked.

"No, I'm headed for Trinidad. I was hoping I might
cut your trail, though. When I did, I intended to drop in
and give you a warning."

"We owe you, and you're welcome to share our camp
tonight," Wyatt said.

"Well, that's neighborly, and I'll accept the invitation.
I'll be glad of the company into Trinidad too, if that's
where you're going. There's talk of a band of Apaches
drifting up from the Turkey Mountains. They might not
get this far north, but they are Jicarilla, and I don't have
to tell you how ornery they can be if they chance up on
a white man."

Wyatt surprised me when he said we'd be happy to
have Buckhorn Smith with us.

"You don't know me, Wyatt Walker," Buckhorn
Smith said, "but I've seen you at work a couple of times.
I watched when Branch Tyler called you out in Fort
Worth." He turned to me then. "This Tyler fella had
just beat up a girl, accused her of stealing his money.
Your pa interfered, and Tyler didn't have enough judgment but to resent it." He looked back at Wyatt. "I was
in the White Elephant in Fort Worth when you had that
game with Doc Holliday. Must have been fifty thousand
dollars on the table at one time. You and Old Doc sure
put on a show that night. Doc had to ride back to Las
Vegas and sell his gambling house."

There was a moment of silence as Buckhorn Smith

seemed to think something over. Then he said, "There is something else I oughta tell you."

"What?" Wyatt asked.

"They know about Abe Scott's map you're supposed to be carrying. They think you're heading for the San Juans to find the source of Abe's gold."

I thought he might ask if Wyatt did have the map, but he didn't. Then Wyatt surprised me.

"I do have the map, Buckhorn, and me and my boy are heading into the mountains. I don't really expect to find any gold, though."

"Well, I'm betting you'll find gold if you look for it. I prospected once with Abe up around Leadville. I never knew him to lie when it came to a strike. I believe he took gold out of the San Juans, and if he says there is still some there, you'll find it. That bunch back there want that map mighty bad too. I was hoping to get that word to you."

"I appreciate it," Wyatt said.

After a moment Buckhorn said he'd better take care of Old Sinner. He got up and led the mule out to where the claybank and the black were pulling at the grass.

"Why did you tell him all that? What do you know about him?" I asked Wyatt.

"Well, I never met him before, but I've heard of him. People always said good things about Buckhorn Smith."

"Do you believe them?"

"I've no reason not to."

"Maybe he'll want to go into the mountains and look for the gold with us," I said. "We could use another man. With Lafe Kennedy knowing about the gold he will surely never give up."

"No, I don't reckon he will. As for inviting Buckhorn

along, I never yet asked a man to take a hand in my troubles just to help me out. Chances are Buckhorn has other fish to fry.''

I liked Buckhorn Smith, and there were all those men on our trail. "I wish you'd ask him. We could give him a share in the gold," I said.

"We can think about it," Wyatt replied.

Chapter Seven

I learned a lot about Buckhorn Smith the next couple of days, and I learned more about Wyatt. They seemed to know most of the famous men of the West. For instance, Buckhorn turned out to know Doc Holliday well. Doc was the Georgia dentist who killed a Negro after the war and had to flee. He took to gambling when he came west. Both Wyatt and Buckhorn told of poker games they'd had with Doc. Both had played in Doc's gambling saloon in Las Vegas, New Mexico Territory.

Buckhorn told of Doc Holliday being chased out of Tucson with the Earps. He said Doc was then in Colorado. He said he was hoping he could get up to Denver and have another game with the famous gambler and gunman.

I had heard stories in Abilene about how many hidden guns Doc carried. Some claimed as many as eleven. I asked Buckhorn about it.

"Doc never carried more than three weapons," he said. "He wore a gun in a hip holster under the right-hand flap of his coat, and he carried another in a shoulder holster under his left arm. The other weapon was a knife in his breast pocket."

"That's all?" I asked, a little disappointed.

"That's all."

But the best recommendation was when I learned that

71

Buckhorn was an admirer of Wild Bill, though the two had never met. I decided that if Buckhorn was interested in going into the mountains with us to look for the old prospector's gold, we surely wanted him along. I told Wyatt that. He still said it was something to think about. Finally, Wyatt did speak to Buckhorn, offering him a share of any gold that was found. Buckhorn said he would consider it.

"What is that?" I asked toward the end of the second day, speaking of a dark blue line that looked like an uneven battlement on the horizon.

Buckhorn, who was riding abreast of me, said, "Them there are the San Juan Mountains."

"The San Juans?"

"The foothills, at least," he confirmed.

That blue line gradually turned lighter as we rode toward it, not the blue of a summer sky, but a smokey, misty blue, reminding me of the last vestiges of smoke from a fire. The flat landscape we had ridden through for weeks paled by comparison as that line of blue seemed to stretch across the world.

When we dipped into a valley, the mountains disappeared altogether, but I knew they were out there. By then I believed something special was going to happen in the mountains. It did, but there were other happenings what were special too.

Before the sun went down, I began to make out individual peaks. On their slopes were the dark green patterns of pines and the dark blue of granite shoulders. A few still wore their caps of white snow, which at times seemed to float against the blue sky, and below these the smoke rose up from the town of Trinidad.

Wyatt pulled up a few miles from the first line of

foothills. Nearby was a spring, some trees, and thick grass. "We'll camp here tonight," he said. "In the morning we'll ride in early and buy supplies. If we're lucky we'll get in and out before the town is stirring too much."

Early next morning we topped a slight rise and looked down on Trinidad. A half dozen streets crisscrossed each other, and the center of town was a collection of stone and brick buildings. A street ran up the slope toward us and turned into a trail about midway up.

"I know a man who runs a mercantile down there," Buckhorn said. "His name is Crockett, and he's a friend of mine. He'll keep his mouth shut about you riding through, Wyatt."

"We'll need something to carry a pack saddle," Wyatt said.

"Art used to keep a few horses. Maybe you can buy a packhorse there."

"You lead us in then, Buckhorn," Wyatt said.

We rode down the slope and into Trinidad. A few people were up and about, but they didn't pay much attention to us. After a while we came to a long, low, adobe building covered with wooden shingles.

"This is Art's place," Buckhorn said.

We swung down, tied our mounts to the hitchrack, and trooped inside.

Two cowboys, a drummer, and a woman were in the store. Another woman, sturdy looking and middle-aged, was behind the counter. She was waiting on the cowboys who stood across the counter from her. They looked as though they had just ridden in from the range. One wore a red checkered shirt and brown canvas pants. The other was dressed in denim pants, blue work shirt, and a brown cowhide vest. Both wore low-heeled, run-over boots. Six-guns swung low on their hips, but there was a look about the guns that suggested they were seldom used.

The drummer sat in a chair beside the stove. He looked us over carefully, maybe eyeing Wyatt longest of all. He wore a checkered suit, a derby hat, and low-cut slippers. I had seen dozens like him in Uncle Ben's hardware store.

The two cowboys stuffed their purchases into a gunnysack and walked past us. Only then did the woman look at us.

"Why, Buckhorn Smith!" she said. "What're you doing in Trinidad?"

"Art got you doing his work for him, Lettie?"

"You ain't heard, then," she said, and her face turned sad.

"Heard what?"

"About Art. He died last winter, Buckhorn."

"I sure am sorry, Lettie. He'll be missed."

"Thank you."

"Now let me introduce those two gents," Buckhorn said. "This here is Wyatt Walker, and this is his son and sidekick, Wes. They've dropped in to buy some supplies."

Buckhorn spoke low, obviously not wanting the drummer who remained beside the stove to hear, and he signaled Lettie Crockett to do the same.

"I've heard of you, Mr. Walker. Heard about your trouble down in El Paso. Them Kennedys came through here a few years back. They made some difficulty for more than a few. You did the world a good turn when you killed two of them. Too bad you didn't finish off Lafe as well. Well, now what can I sell you?"

Wyatt gave her his list, and she began to gather the items on the counter.

All the while that drummer kept his eyes on Wyatt. After a moment, he got up, crossed the store, and went out. He gave Wyatt another long look as he passed.

"I think he recognized you," Buckhorn said.

"Maybe, but there is no help for it now," Wyatt answered. "Who was he, Mrs. Crockett?"

"Nat Ford. He comes through every two or three months. I don't like him much, but sometimes we have to do business with him."

She was stacking goods on the counter as she talked. Buckhorn had begun to help her.

"Buckhorn said your husband used to sell horses. I wonder if you still do. I need one to carry a pack," Wyatt said.

"There's some in the corral out back. They're twenty dollars a piece. Go through the back door and you can see them. Pick out the one you want."

Buckhorn stayed behind to help her gather our supplies. I thought he was enjoying the work mightily. He hadn't said if he was going with us into the San Juans. As I watched him with Miss Lettie, I began to doubt he would. He seemed awfully interested in helping her out.

"I think Buckhorn has his eye on that widow woman," I said to Wyatt as we stepped outside to look at the horses.

Wyatt smiled. "Maybe he just found something more interesting to do than ride with us."

The ponies shied to the back of the corral when we approached. They didn't look like much to me, but Wyatt said they looked fine for pack animals. He looked them over. Then he slipped through the poles and walked in among them, stirring them up. He stopped near a scruffy-looking mare with stubby legs and studied her. Then he went inside a small shed and came out with a hackamore. Slipping the halter over her head, he led her outside.

"When you're buying a horse, the first thing you check is their teeth," he said. "If they're worn, the horse is getting old." He held the mare's lips apart to show her teeth. "What do you think?" he asked.

"They look all right to me."

"You're right. They're in good shape."

"How old is she?"

"Between five and seven."

He checked her hooves, testing the shoes on each to make sure they were secure and not too worn. When he was finished, he said, "She'll carry our load easily enough."

"She won't run very fast," I said.

"You don't buy a packhorse for speed. Look at those shoulders. Look at her legs. What you want is a horse that can pack a load."

I followed Wyatt and the mare around the store to the front. When we rounded the corner, Wyatt pulled up short. A half-dozen men were collected across the street. They stood in a small knot, their eyes on the front of Crockett's store. Nat Ford, the drummer, sat on his sample case among them. The look on his face was one of anticipation, like he'd just bought a ticket to a rodeo.

One man stood a little before the others. He was a fancy dresser, serge instead of denim, and he wore two well-polished six-guns. I tried to see his face, but he wore the flat-crowned, broad-brimmed hat well down.

Buckhorn came from the store. He was carrying a packframe, and he placed that beside our supplies. Wyatt, who after that first look seemed to ignore the growing crowd, crossed to Buckhorn.

"I saw them gathering," Buckhorn said. "I told Lettie I had to get you out of here." He spoke as they strapped the packframe on the mare and began to load the supplies.

"Who is the kid?" Wyatt asked.

"Mace Cantrell. His family is big hereabouts. Mace fancies himself a fast gun. Lettie says he's out to make a reputation for himself, but I'm hoping he won't push you."

"I expect he will," Wyatt said, his voice already hard.

Wyatt had returned the Colt he'd given me back to his warbag. I began to wish I still had it, for I could feel there was trouble coming.

The crowd built to as many as twenty men. When Wyatt and Buckhorn had the pack mare loaded, Wyatt went inside to settle up with Lettie Crockett.

"Are you going with us, Buckhorn?" I asked.

"I don't think so, Wes," he said. "Lettie has asked me to stay on here a spell and help her in the store. I told her I would. I might ride up there and check on you before winter sets in, that is, if I'd be welcome."

"You'd be welcome. You know that."

Wyatt came out and stood beside the horses. Mace Cantrell stepped into the street.

"I'm told you're Wyatt Walker, the gunfighter," he shouted from across the street.

"Get Wes inside, Buckhorn," Wyatt said.

"Are you denying you're Wyatt Walker, mister?" Cantrell called out again.

"I'm Walker."

A change came over Wyatt. The skin on his face grew

tight, and his eyes seemed to grow larger. His mouth was a thin line across his face.

"Come on, Wes," Buckhorn said. Taking my shoulder, he propelled me toward the store. When we reached the door, he pushed me inside. He stopped in the doorway beside Lettie, where they could watch what was about to happen together.

I went to a window.

Mace Cantrell walked out into the street. He seemed to measure the distance between himself and Wyatt, stopping when they were about thirty feet apart.

"I'm calling you, Walker," he said.

He stood in a little crouch, his feet maybe twelve inches apart, his hands hovering a little above the butts of the two fancy guns. I could see his face now. He didn't look to be more than twenty. He had deep sideburns down his temples and a fuzzy-looking blond mustache across his upper lip. There was a cocky set to the expression on his face, but I saw him lick his lips.

My mouth and throat were cottony, but I didn't move. I guess I might have wondered what was to happen to me if Wyatt was killed, but I don't remember. I don't recall I thought of Wyatt, either. Maybe I didn't think of anything. Maybe I was just caught up in what was about to happen out there in the dusty street.

"I'm just passing through, Cantrell," Wyatt said. "I stopped in to buy supplies. I have my boy with me. You back off, and I'll take him and ride out of here."

"You've heard of me then," Cantrell said, and that cocky look seemed to intensify.

"Only just now, but I'm told you have family here. Back off from this fight and go and join them. Let me ride out."

"You can't talk me out of it, Walker."

"I wish I could."

"Draw, Walker!"

The crowd parted fast at that. A few shouted encouragement to Cantrell. Nat Ford still sat on his sample case. He was leaning forward, his hands on his knees, mesmerized by the unfolding scene.

"So be it," Wyatt said.

I was watching Cantrell when it happened. His hands made a quick dive, but the single shot rang out about the time they reached his guns. I looked at Wyatt. The Colt was in his hand, a wisp of smoke curling up from the end of the barrel.

My eyes went back to Cantrell. He seemed to look up into the sky, as the sun struck him square in the face. I saw his lips move, but I didn't hear what he said. Maybe he didn't say anything, just worked his lips, wishing he could speak.

Then his hands left the butts of his still-holstered guns and crept up to his chest. He seemed to shudder a few times before he folded and went down, still clutching his chest, crumpling there in the dust like a weed drenched in boiling water. Then his lanky body somehow stretched itself out.

I looked back at Wyatt. He watched Cantrell's prone body for a moment. Then he put the Colt away.

I felt Buckhorn's hand on my shoulder. "I didn't intend for you to watch that boy, but maybe it's good you did. You'll never see a faster draw."

I couldn't speak. I had just seen my first man die, and it seemed to me the earth should have shook a little. Instead, the only thing I could see moving were specks of dust caught in the sunbeams that poured through the glass window. It just looked too easy to do.

"I didn't see it, Buckhorn," I mumbled finally. "I was watching Cantrell."

We went outside, Buckhorn pushing me along before him. "You two git on them hosses and hightail it out of here," he said to Wyatt, and he literally picked me up and sat me astride the claybank.

"I'll need to make a statement to the law," Wyatt said.

"I told you how big the Cantrells are around here, Wyatt. If you don't take your boy and git, he's apt to witness his pa's lynching. Lettie and I will make the proper statements to the marshal."

Wyatt looked at me. "Were you watching?" he asked.

"Yes, sir."

"I'm sorry."

"You tried to get out of it."

"Head north out of town," Buckhorn said. "It'll throw them off in case someone tries to chase you. You can head into the mountains later on."

Wyatt gathered the black's reins and climbed up. His movements were slow, and he looked tired and a lot older.

I looked down at Cantrell's body as we passed. His eyes were open, and I thought they seemed to follow me. His blood made a dark circle in the street.

Wyatt kept the slow pace through town as if not to suggest pursuit to the crowd of Cantrell cronies. When I looked back, they were standing around, some of them looking after us, like they were trying to make up their minds what to do.

We cleared the houses and went over a little rise, and

Wyatt put the black into a run. Not all out, for there was the packhorse, but enough to put a little distance between us and the town while the men back there decided.

A couple of miles out we pulled up. They were just clearing the edge of town, a dozen or more riders, and they were stirring up quite a tail of dust.

Wyatt tossed me the pack mare's lead rope. "Keep heading north," he said. "Get as much speed out of her as you can without wearing her down completely."

"What're you gonna do?" I asked.

"Whatever I have to that will convince them to head back to town."

"I want that extra Colt you carry," I said.

He brought it from a saddlebag and gave it to me buttfirst, saying, "Don't use it but to defend yourself, and don't turn back when you hear shooting. I'll catch up to you pretty soon."

I didn't answer, just tucked the gun into my belt and headed out. To tell the truth, though, I was getting plenty wearied of being chased. Lafe Kennedy had tracked us clear across Kansas, indeed, might still be on our trail. Now a dozen riders were after us because Mace Cantrell was foolish enough to force a face-off, hoping to make a reputation for himself. I asked myself where the justice was in it all.

Wyatt didn't wait for them there, but each time I looked back, he had fallen farther behind. I figured he was waiting for a likely place to make a stand if the riders kept coming. I wondered how I could keep from turning back to help out when the shooting started, for after that fight, and though he had killed Cantrell, I was seeing him in a different light. When he had looked at me, I saw death in his eyes, another kind of dying than that on the features of Cantrell, but death all the same.

I kept riding north, the mountains to my left. The day was clear, and the rugged peaks seemed to peer down at me. They looked near enough for me to toss a rock among them, but I knew better. I had learned something about distances from living in Kansas all my life.

They held a fascination for me from the first, those mountains. They looked like a jagged row of monstrous teeth rising out of the earth, some of them white-capped, others with bare rocky peaks, their lower slopes cloaked with pines, except for a bare shoulder of granite now and then. They seemed to offer themselves as a haven where a man could lose himself, and I think I understood better then the look I had seen on Wyatt's face a few times when he talked of us wintering there.

Not till I rode off and left Wyatt behind did I realize how tired I was. I was not only tired of being chased. I wanted to get somewhere and rest. I wanted to think about something other than what would happen if we were caught. I wanted to spend a day just lying in the shade of a tree. I wanted to enjoy the claybank and Wyatt without thinking that every day with them might be the last. But none of that would happen unless Wyatt scared off that bunch back there.

I think I understood what Wyatt had been feeling. He had been running since the shooting in El Paso. In other times, he would have stopped and shot it out with Kennedy. But in El Paso he had reached a watershed. He had come to terms with the death of Sue Ellen and determined he would straighten out his relationship with me.

But would he change again? How long would it be

before he turned on Kennedy and had it out, just as he was about to do with the bunch back there? I took a deep breath at the thought of what might happen then.

I pondered that as I rode, as well as the ugly scene back there in Trinidad where Mace Cantrell's blood had wet the dusty street. I had seen my first gunfight, and somehow showdowns like that didn't seem to hold the adventure of the stories I had listened to on the streets of Abilene.

The country was full of pines. I crossed a well-used road with a sign saying the road led to the Orpheus Coal Mine. Beyond that the terrain turned hilly, and I began to climb, a few low hills first and then taller ones. At the summit of one I gave the horses a rest and looked back to see if Wyatt was still back there, but he had disappeared among the pines, nor could I spot any dust. I sat there for ten minutes or more watching and listening before I sent the claybank down the opposite slope.

Awhile later I heard shooting. The pop of the guns sounded way off, the echoes tapping gently and distantly against the mountains. I considered riding back, but I knew the issue would long have been settled. Pretty soon there were no more shots, and I headed north again, slower now, for I wanted Wyatt to catch up.

I never considered he might not come. That's how much confidence I was gaining in him. Not long afterward he rode in. I was stopped to let the horses drink from a little stream that tumbled down a hillside. The black drank heavily as I studied Wyatt's face, reading nothing there.

"What happened?" I asked.

"They weren't very serious. A few close shots tamed their tempers. They beat it back to town."

"Will it end here?"

"As far as that bunch is concerned."

"Was the marshal among them?"

"I didn't see a star. I think these might have been just a few of Cantrell's buddies who were feeling some guilt they had egged him on. They felt they had to do something for show. But if Cantrell's folks are as powerful as Buckhorn said, they might offer a reward. If it's big enough, that might bring a bounty hunter in."

I thought of Kennedy. Now he might get paid to hunt Wyatt down.

"Will we be heading into the mountains now?" I asked.

"Sometime tomorrow," he said. "For now we'll just keep riding north."

Chapter Eight

The mountains were spectacular. The glimpses I'd had stirred my imagination but didn't prepare me for actually riding among them. Often I pulled the claybank up to enjoy some scene, a tall peak girded with the green of the pines, higher up the rugged shoulders, and then the giant finger that seemed to pierce the sky. The colors on the cliffs were dazzling. They came in patterns of rust, pink, black, and grays, and there were always many shades of blue. I didn't seem able to get enough of standing on a summit and gradually letting my eyes roam over some view that unfolded mile after mile.

Once we gazed down and watched a grizzly with one-year-old cubs feed across a meadow. The season was well into summer, and the bears had filled out. As they moved, sunlight reflected off shiny coats as the wind stirred black lines along their fur. They seemed to epitomize wildness.

But there were times when I was apprehensive. Traveling through narrow canyons whose sheer granite walls climbed to spectacular heights had me to thinking of being trapped there.

The mood of those dark canyons was a perfect fit for the face Wyatt wore most of the time. I figured he was thinking about what had happened back in Trinidad, the killing of Cantrell and the fact that I'd been there to see it. But how he could fault himself for what had happened was beyond me. Mace Cantrell had forced the issue. Sooner or later I knew we would have to talk about it. I just couldn't see myself as the one to bring it up.

We were in the mountains a week before Wyatt mentioned the affair. We camped along a creek, caught fish, and cooked them for supper. The sun was just set, the last color pulled from the sky, and a few stars were out. The grass was thick and green, and the sound of the horses pulling at it was like music you're only half aware of. There had been no sign of pursuit, either by a posse from Trinidad or by the Kennedy gang, and it looked like we were free of both.

"Would you like to hear about the first man I ever killed?" he suddenly asked, his voice a little tight at the memory, or at the need to speak of it to me.

He sat across the fire, his face cloaked in shadows and a two-day growth of beard. The dancing flames reflected in his eyes. I had heard the story of that first killing many times, and I would have welcomed the chance to hear him tell of it a few days earlier. But since seeing Mace Cantrell lying in the street I wasn't sure I wanted to listen.

"I would," I said and hoped he hadn't noticed my hesitation.

He was quiet for a moment, seeming to collect his thoughts. "It was a few months after I dropped you off in Abilene," he began. "I found myself in Austin, then in Jacksboro, then San Antonio. Next I drifted back to Fort Worth and spent some time in the White Elephant. I was gambling heavy by then and winning enough to pay my way. But I was getting a reputation and finding it harder and harder to find a game.

"Then I heard about a new place which had opened up. It was far out on the frontier on the Clear Fork of the Brazos River near where Collins Creek flows into it. There had been a lot of Indian trouble out there, and a new fort had just opened up, Fort Griffin it was called. I decided to try my luck there.

"The fort was on a hill, and at the foot of the hill was the Flat, never called anything but that as far as I know. There was just a jumble of houses built from green lumber and a passel of tents along a single street. Any empty space was filled with ricks of buffalo hides that still smelled to high heaven.

"There was plenty of action, however. Ranchers from two hundred miles around came in for supplies, sometimes bringing a gang of cowboys who were looking for fun, rough fun, at that. An army of buffalo hunters were making it their headquarters at the time—men as rough as any I ever came across. Some hadn't bathed for years and bragged about it. Any man who took offense at their odor and showed it had to fight.

"The buffalo hunters didn't carry six-guns, but they did carry long, wicked-looking hunting knives and their Sharps .50-caliber, rifles, rifles said to knock down a buffalo at 800 yards. In fact, the story going around at the time was of the recent fight at Adobe Walls in the Panhandle. Bat Masterson was quoted as having seen a hunter knock an Indian from his horse at 1,000 yards. That shot made the Indians back off, Quanah Parker among them, though the hunters were outnumbered maybe 500 to one.

"Well, I was in a game in one of the temporary tent saloons when a commotion began in the street. Bullets whipped through the top of the tent, and everyone fell to the floor and lay as flat as they could. A woman called Nasty Nell was crouched behind the bar. The shooting died down, and she stood up. At that moment, the shooting commenced again. A .50-caliber bullet caught her.

"I wasn't enjoying the games there. I wasn't enjoying what my life had become. I certainly wasn't enjoying the shooting. Suddenly, I just stood up and walked outside. A man called Hurricane Bill stood in the street. He was taking potshots at anything that moved. I later learned he'd had some trouble over a woman with another hunter named O'Brien. Well, he turned and saw me and cut down. The bullet whipped past my face. I drew and shot him through the heart."

He stopped talking, and I sat there a moment and waited for him to go on. When he didn't, I said, "It was a nervy thing you did."

"I didn't do it to be admired," he said.

"You did it because he killed Nasty Nell . . . because he would have surely killed you with his next shot."

"I did it because he missed me."

"Because he missed you?" I asked him, and I was startled at the thought.

"You see, I went out there wanting him to do to me what he had done to Nell. When he didn't, I drew my gun and killed him."

"You had just seen Nasty Nell blasted, and you wanted to die too?"

"Wanted it the worst kind."

I had heard Aunt Mamie and Uncle Ben say it was death he was seeking when he left Abilene. I don't think I ever believed it till I heard Wyatt say it himself.

"Because of Sue Ellen," I said.

"And because of you . . . because I'd run off and left you."

I sat there and savored that for a moment, trying to fit it together into some kind of pattern, and I wondered what his need to tell me had to do with the killing of Mace Cantrell, and us heading off into the mountains and away from Lafe Kennedy so we could get to know each other better. I just couldn't make sense of it.

Then he said, "When I came to myself after killing Hurricane Bill, I would have done anything to undo it. When I shot Cantrell back there, I didn't feel a thing."

"You acted like you felt it," I said.

"That was because you saw it. I hated I did it before you, and because of my promise to Mamie. I was afraid you would think it was something big, something to admire. You've been asking a lot of questions and doing a lot of talking about gunfighters with Buckhorn and me. I thought you seeing me kill Cantrell might be the first step toward your turning out like me. I've been watching you . . . wondering if that was true."

"Did you make up your mind?" I asked.

"I think so. I think it may have worked just the opposite on you."

"I don't think I could hear about another gunfight without seeing Mace Cantrell in the street," I said, "and I won't ever forget the sight of his blood in the hot sun."

His eyes bored into mine. I had the feeling he was reading my soul. Then he said, "Mamie and Ben did a good job raising you up."

The campfire was dying down, and I could barely see his face. I had the feeling he had just talked to me as he had to no other person. There was the impression he had emptied everything out before me and was void inside.

From the slope above a wolf howled. I shivered and didn't know if I was cold because of the dying fire, the sounds of the wolf, or the bowed head of Wyatt. Other wolves answered the first, and they seemed to be gathering. They went quiet then, but I could see them in my mind's eye as they silently gave chase.

I yearned to say something to him. And because I couldn't find the words to speak, I think I felt for that moment a little of the bleakness in his life when he lost the woman he loved. Suddenly, I was filled with desolation that I had never known my mother, and that I might never get to know Wyatt, though he sat before me in the flesh.

"There is a new holster for the extra Colt in the pack," Wyatt said. "There is also a new Winchester."

"Did you buy enough cartridges for me to practice some?" I asked.

"I bought plenty."

"When can I start?"

"Anytime you want."

He was silent. A coal snapped, shooting out to start some dry grass burning. Wyatt put it out with his boot.

"You'll be carrying those guns from now on," he said when he was sitting again, "and there is something I'll say to you."

"What?"

"Don't ever use them on another man if you don't have to."

"You keep saying that, but how will I know?"

"You'll know. At least, I think you will. Most men of judgment do, and you've already shown me you've got that. It's like any passion, Wes. Killing, eating, drinking too much . . . can get you by the throat and lead you through life. Men with judgment discipline their passions with moderation. That's the key.'' His voice was as intense as the pile of red coals I was staring into.

I looked across at him. I couldn't see him very well, but the air above the fire seemed charged with some kind of energy that flowed across from him to me. I knew then that Wyatt Walker, the man who fathered me, had just confessed to me the rule he now wished he'd lived his life by. The rule was moderation. I took it to heart that night, telling myself it was something I'd try to practice.

Our blankets were already spread. Without further comment, Wyatt slipped off his boots and crawled between his. Soon his even breathing reached me across the fire. I sat there awhile longer and wondered if I would ever be able to understand him.

On the high slopes the wolves still ran, the sounds of the chase distant now, distant but nonetheless real. I went to my blankets, yanked off my boots, and went to bed. I felt drained, but not from the long ride that day, but the total and complete way I had identified with what Wyatt had been trying to impart to me. Not that I understood it all—still don't, I expect.

Chapter Nine

By now we were following Abe Scott's map. Wyatt took it out often to study it. I don't think his mind was on what we might find at that final mark, however. Following the map was just our way of getting into the mountains.

Foremost in my mind was putting miles between us and Trinidad. I wanted to find some place where we would be safe from Kennedy as well as any posse that might search for us.

I don't believe I thought there would be any gold at the end of the ride. But I couldn't help but toy with the possibility, thinking of the things you could do with it. Of course, a man wrestling with his soul, as Wyatt was, had other things to think about.

The thought hit me that Lafe Kennedy might be bought off with gold if we got to it before he caught up with us. I wasn't so sure about the Cantrells. After all, they were rich anyway. But even if they couldn't be bought off with money there were places a man could go and not be found.

We could live under a different name. Men in the West did it all the time. Uncle Ben had once told me that half the men in Abilene might now possess different names than what they were given at birth . . . a lot of women too. San Francisco came to mind. We could go there and lose ourselves. We could bring Aunt Mamie and Uncle Ben out for visits. Life in San Francisco wouldn't be bad. Or we could live someplace in the east until Wyatt's fame faded. There were numerous possibilities, and I may have begun to set my heart on finding the gold after all.

There came a time when I lost count of the days. I just knew that summer would soon be half gone, and we were still climbing and traveling west. The miles we were covering didn't slip past easily, either. Some days I could look back from the top of some bluff and see our campsite of the previous night.

Often we trailed up slopes too steep to ride; stepping down, we pulled ourselves up, leading the horses along behind. Much of the time we rode over solid rock. Obviously, we weren't going to be easy to find.

In time I began to feel there was no one else in the world except the two of us. I found myself wondering if any man had ever traveled there before us. Of course, I knew they had, for we were following the map and finding the landmarks. Then I spotted charcoal from a campfire. I was so startled I pulled up to study what remained of an obvious camp.

"What have you found?" Wyatt asked, swinging the black around.

"Did you see this?"

"I saw it."

"Who could it have been?"

"There are hoofprints. Do they tell you anything?"

They were faint, had been exposed to wind, but they were clear enough to be read.

"See anything different about them?"

"No."

"Look closer."

I looked in vain.

"Those horses weren't shod," he said.

"Indians?" For the moment I forgot all about Lafe Kennedy and the Cantrells.

"Arapaho or maybe Apache. The Arapaho are to the north, the Jicarilla Apaches are to the south. The two tribes do some trading back and forth. Sometimes they raid each other for horses and women."

"How far are we from the end of Abe Scott's map?" I asked.

"Not far."

"I hope it's far enough we won't be getting visits from either tribe. I don't want to spend the winter worrying about my hair."

Wyatt laughed, which was a sign he was shaking his black mood. Then he said, "They might admire your hair at that. It's getting long enough. Someday soon I'll cut it for you."

The chance of us encountering Indians was no joke to me. I grew up on tales of what Comanches and Kiowa did to settlers and traders when the first whites pushed onto the plains. The Indians had used every trick they knew to keep whites out. They had failed, but the fight they waged had been terrible and bloody.

"Indians are usually friendly till you give them reason not to be," Wyatt said, reading my mind.

"I'll take your word for it."

"Chances of us seeing any are slim. They won't be traveling up here after the snow flies. They'll be tucked away in some canyon or valley."

"Good. Thoughts of Kennedy and the Cantrells are enough for me to deal with this winter."

We continued to find the landmarks on Scott's map. Usually, a day's travel separated them, sometimes two. We passed the granite-faced cliff, the cave, and finally there was only left the lonesome pine. My expectations began to build when I thought we were nearing it. Then one day we topped out into a shallow alpine valley where a small lake lay like a mirror at the lowest point.

"This is it," Wyatt said.

"I don't see the pine."

"Over there. Before the cliff."

I saw it then, a single pine against the gray granite of the cliff. "How could it survive the winter up this high?" I asked.

"Who knows. A freak of nature, maybe. Maybe the cliff protects it. Anyway, if Abe Scott wasn't totally fooling, we should find where he mined for gold somewhere along that cliff."

"He didn't say exactly where?" I asked.

"Afraid not, and I reckon I wasn't interested enough to ask him."

"Guess we're in for a treasure hunt."

"There'll be plenty of time for that later on. What you and I have to do first is get ready for winter."

"What do we have to do?"

"We have to build a cabin unless we find a cave we can live in. A cave would be warmer. Then we have to get in our winter meat, but we can't live off of meat only. We'll gather nuts and berries and make Indian pemmican. We'll harvest a good store of roots as well. We'll need some hay for the horses. They'll dig for grass under the snow till it gets too deep. After that we'll have to feed them."

"When do we start?" I asked.

He studied the sun before he spoke. "We'll ride that cliff looking for a cave. Maybe we'll find one. If we don't, we'll locate a good spot for a permanent camp. Maybe beside the lake down there near the trees. But we won't work today. We'll settle into camp, cook supper, and get a good night's rest."

"How long before snow?" I asked.

"I figure we have a month, maybe a little longer if we're lucky, but snow comes early up here, and we mustn't depend on luck."

"How much snow?"

"Twenty feet or more this high up. It won't be easy to move around in, but we'll make us some snowshoes and manage."

That much snow was hard for me to imagine. Twenty feet was more than three times Wyatt's height. Wintering in the mountains began to take on different dimensions for me.

Wyatt sent the black toward the cliff. I followed.

"Save us a lot of time if we find a cave," I said to his back.

We began our search from east to west along the cliff. From a distance the cliff had appeared sheer and uncluttered, but that had been misleading. Fields of large boulders and jagged rocks were embedded in the ground before it, and they dribbled out for several yards.

Some of the rocks were as tall as a house, and they were so close together at times we had trouble finding a passage for the horses. We hadn't been able to make out the rocks from the valley's rim because they were the same color as the cliff. They formed a natural barrier, and as we worked our way through, I found myself thinking a cave situated behind them would be easy to defend, an indication of how I had begun to think after being chased across Kansas by the Kennedy gang.

About halfway along the cliff and still some distance from the pine, we came out in a small clearing. It was no more than a half acre in size, and the surprising thing was the thick carpet of grass. Four or five aspens and firs grew around the edges as well.

"There has to be water in here. Let's see if we can find it," Wyatt said.

We found it near the base of the cliff, a thin stream that circled the foundation of a tall, wide boulder that rose many feet up the cliff. We followed the water into the narrow passage that separated the boulder from the cliff and found its source, a crack in the cliff maybe six inches off the ground. It emptied into a shallow pool and then trickled off to circle the boulder.

"Well, look at that," Wyatt said.

It wasn't the water he pointed to. Several feet farther on was an opening in the cliff tall enough for a man to stand in.

"Maybe we won't have to build a cabin," I said.

Stepping down, we drop-reined the horses and walked to the opening. Wyatt stopped there and began to sniff.

"What?" I asked.

"A bear," he said. "His smell is faint, but he's been here not too long ago."

"You don't think he's still in there, do you?"

"I doubt it. Not this far into summer. He probably wintered here."

Returning to the black, Wyatt drew the Winchester from its boot. When he came back, he said, "You stay out here. If it looks promising, I'll give you a call. If you hear a shot, you better back off and give me room.

I'll be coming out with a bear on my tail. On second thought, maybe you should hold the horses. I'd hate to come out and find myself on foot.''

I didn't just hold them. I climbed into the claybank's saddle to wait. There was the soft sound of the water coming from the cliff and from somewhere in the valley I heard the caw of a crow. The sun seemed to pour down harder there among the rocks, making it warmer than it had been outside in the valley. I thought of the winter and twenty feet of snow and wondered what it would feel like when snow covered most of the rocks. But it was a snug place, and I decided again that it would be a location easy to defend.

Then Wyatt called.

I found him just inside. He stood in the front of what was more like a cavern than a cave. The large chamber was maybe fifty feet deep and twice as wide. There was a surprising amount of light, and glancing up, I saw the source. Three holes fifty or so feet up allowed the light to spill in. I had the feeling I was in a barn whose roof had three huge holes.

''The smoke from our fire will escape through them,'' Wyatt said.

''We're going to live here then?'' I asked.

''Why not? Abe Scott did. He had his fire over there, and he left us some firewood.''

I walked to a small pit and looked down on a hole still filled with ash. Scott had done his cooking there, and he had left the rocks on which he had set his pots. There were two much larger rocks. I figured he had used them as a chair and a table.

''What about the bear?'' I asked.

''I don't think we'll share. He'll have to find another

place to spend the winter.'' Wyatt pointed to the wall to the left of the entrance. ''Abe isn't the only man to spend time here,'' he said.

Several drawings had been carved into the wall. One was of a buffalo, another a deer, the others of smaller animals. There were arrows and other marks as though someone might have counted off the days. They were pictures a child might have drawn, crude, but they had power.

''Who did them?'' I asked.

''Indians,'' Wyatt said, ''probably a long time ago. I've seen such drawings before. I heard a man say once the Indians called those who made the drawings ancient ones.''

''Too bad the water doesn't run through here,'' I said.

''We wouldn't have to go out in the cold come winter.''

''Maybe you'd like a café too. You could order them to bring your breakfast in.''

''I wouldn't mind.''

''We can do a few things to make it comfortable,'' he said. ''We'll need a table and a couple of benches. We can build them from split logs and pegs. We might want to build us a better stove to cook on. There's probably soapstone out there at the lake. It hardens when it dries. With all that we'll spend less time than if we had to build a cabin, and we'll be warmer in here as well.''

''What about the horses?'' I asked.

''We'll bring them inside when the worst of winter comes. There's plenty of room. They'll smell the place up a little, but I never minded a barn smell. How about you?''

"Never," I said, grateful the claybank would be out of the snow and close.

"We'll move our supplies in this afternoon," Wyatt said. "But I think we'll sleep outside while it's warm."

That suited me, for I had learned to love waking up at night with a view of a star-filled sky and the noise of the night—and the knowledge that Wyatt slept nearby.

Chapter Ten

"Here, strap it on," Wyatt said, presenting me with the new holster.

We had set up our camp and ate an early supper. The late afternoon sun seemed to be resting for a moment on one of the peaks to the west. A cool wind was sweeping the valley, even touching down in the compound before the cave, where we planned to live until we moved inside for the winter.

I held the holster out before me a moment, enjoying the new smell of the leather. Then placing it around my waist, I buckled it up and settled it on my hips. Wyatt tested its fit by slipping a hand beneath it.

"Tighten it another notch," he said. "You don't want it slipping down or twisting about from the weight of the gun. You'll want to treat it with some tallow, but I'll show you how to do that later on."

When I had the holster strapped on, I checked where my hand came when my arm was hanging free.

"Where did you learn that?" he asked.

"I've seen you do it."

He didn't say anything to that, but he did produce the extra Colt, giving it to me buttfirst as always.

I slipped it into the holster.

It was the first gun I ever owned, and I felt like the moment was special . . . like I had become a man. But I

already knew that it takes a lot more than a gun to make
a man.

I felt awkward at first. I was aware of the weight, and
the belt and holster restricted my movement, not to mention the feel of the gun against my thigh. But Wyatt said
the only way to get used to it was to keep it on. He also
said I should wear it every time I went out.

We walked out to shoot, and I began by lifting the
gun about even with my shoulder, aimed at a turf of
grass, and squeezed the trigger. The bullet landed a couple of feet beyond the grass.

"You let the gun jump," Wyatt said. "You have to
hold it steady, and you don't aim like that."

"What do you do then?"

"Just lift it and let the barrel be an extension of your
hand. Let it be like a finger. There's a natural coordi-
nation between the hand and the eyes that will do the
aiming for you. Just eye the spot where you want the
bullet to go. Holding the gun steady is the hard part.
Anticipation of the shot is apt to make the hand jerk a
little when the explosion comes. You'll get used to it
with practice."

"How do I learn a fast draw?" I asked.

"You don't . . . not for a while. Accuracy comes first.
After you can hit what you shoot at, and handling the
gun becomes pretty much a habit, you can practice speed
on the draw. By then the moves will have become almost
automatic . . . like the strike of a snake. If you have the
right reflexes, speed will come. If you don't, you can
practice the rest of your life, and you'll still be slow."

"Was your draw natural? Buckhorn said I'd never see
one faster."

"It's natural."

When he spoke, he didn't look at me, but out over the rocks to the east. There was no brag in his voice. Just the opposite. I found myself wondering what kind of life he might have lived if the speed of his draw had been more like that of other men.

"How often can I practice?"

"Winter will be here before we know it. We have a lot to do if we lay in enough food for us and the horses before then. If we don't get it done, spring is apt to come without us. But we'll find a little time for you to work with the gun. But always have it with you outside."

"Why? I think we may be free of Kennedy and his gang and the Cantrells for a while."

"Maybe, but there's the bear. He might come skulking around. They don't usually attack a man, but they've been known to if they are hungry enough. You wouldn't be able to kill him with a six-gun unless you got mighty lucky, but the noise from a shot would scare him off.

"If you do spot him, leave him alone unless he pushes you. Just don't let him get too close. If he does, the sound of the shot might cause him to rush you instead of making him run. You just remember that a bear is fast the first hundred yards. I've seen them run down a deer at that distance. You don't want to have to match speeds with him."

"But bears can't see very well."

"No, but they make up for that with their nose. There may not be another animal with a bear's ability to smell. If the wind is right, they'll know you're about even over long distances. He can come up on you, and you won't even know he's around.

"Bears are curious too. They've been known to slip into a man's camp at night to keep tabs on what's happening there. You probably won't know he's been around till he's gone.''

"You make it sound as if bears are human.''

"Don't sell them short . . . them nor any other animal.''

"We'll be together most of the time, won't we?'' I asked uneasily.

"Most of the time, but in the beginning I want you to cut hay for the horses.''

"What will you be doing?''

"I'll be hunting. When I come in, we'll butcher out the meat and start it to curing. Hopefully, we'll have some time to make the cave a little more comfortable. If we work hard, there might still be time to do some shooting each day before dark.''

I thought Wyatt had the best of the work. I'd never cut hay, but I'd seen it done. Hunting seemed a lot more fun. I didn't say anything, though. I had already learned there was a good purpose behind anything Wyatt suggested. Probably, he'd be able to kill more meat if I wasn't along.

"I never cut hay,'' I said. "And even if I knew how, we don't have a scythe.''

He took out his bowie and walked a few feet out to where there was grass. Twisting the tops of the stems together, he held them with his left hand. With his right he made a sweep with the knife. "Like that,'' he said. "And when you have a bundle about the size of your thigh, tie it off with a good tough stem. Lay it in the sun to cure. When it's ready, we'll move it inside the cave.''

Thinking of the bear, I said, "You mentioned you had a Winchester for me. Shouldn't I have it with me when I'm out there cutting hay?''

''The Colt will be enough for now. I don't want to load you down with guns.''

He didn't ride the black when he went out to hunt next morning, but he did take the mare to haul back his kill. I watched him circle the lake and disappear to the south. My last view of him and the mare was when they disappeared into some aspen along the foot of a bluff.

I remembered Wyatt saying there might be trout in the lake, so I rigged a line before I went out to do my haying.

Before I began to cut the hay, I baited the hook with a moth, tossed the line out, and tied it off to a bush in the edge of the water. Then I set about my work.

I had several shocks cut and tied before I remembered to check my fish line. It was tight when I walked down for a look. I pulled in a fair-sized trout. I strung the fish on a limber switch and left him in enough water to keep him alive, weighting the switch down with a rock to keep him from getting away. I caught three more before I took the line out.

Wyatt was right about the grass around the lake. It grew tall and sweet and was easy to cut. I worked hard with the sun warm on my back.

Surprisingly, I found myself enjoying the work. I had worked in the hardware store for Uncle Ben before, which wasn't bad, but I hadn't seen the purpose behind it, except to help out. But cutting the hay had a clear purpose. It would keep my horse alive come winter. That thought gave my efforts all meaning in the world.

The meadow was awash with the smell of new curing hay when Wyatt led the mare in. He stopped and looked at the laid out bundles. ''A few more mornings like this and the horses will fare well this winter,'' he said.

His praise was like a tonic, but I tried not to show it. "You scored too," I said, indicating the buck tied across the mare's back.

"We'll dress him out after we cook and eat," he said.

"How about fish?"

"Fish?"

I walked to the water and held up my catch. "I'll clean if you'll cook."

"Maybe I've had better offers, but I don't remember them," he said.

As we walked toward the compound behind the line of rocks, I carried a lot of pride in my heart. There was the feeling I was making a contribution to our welfare. There was the satisfaction too that I wore Wyatt's gift on my hip, and it wasn't just that he had given me the gun. It was that he trusted me with it.

I guess it's the sharing of such things that brings people close . . . that strengthens the bonds between them. It's a day I'll long remember.

"I'm glad I came with you, Pa," I said, and the words just slipped out.

He looked at me and smiled.

I sat on a rock and watched as he cooked the trout. I think I noticed for the first time how swift, confident, and precise were his moves. There were no wasted motions . . . like in the draw he was so famous for.

"Did you see anything of the bear while I was out?" he asked, his back to me.

"No, sir."

"You keep a sharp watch. I saw his sign up the valley a ways. It was fresh. He knows we're here. He was snooping around last night."

"What did you see?"

"Tracks. They were as big as any I ever saw. He'll go well over a thousand pounds. He's a male and old too. They get mean sometimes when something comes into their territory. We have to be careful of him. He might come in for the horses one night."

I stood up. "Maybe we ought to stand guard."

"We'll start bringing them into the compound soon. Till then we'll keep a close watch. I expect they'll catch his smell if he comes around. The black will wake me up."

The idea that the bear might come in for the claybank left me mighty uneasy. That horse had become pet, playmate, and brother. Losing him was something I didn't want to contemplate.

"I want you to let me have the rifle you bought for me," I told Wyatt.

He seemed to know why I asked for it. "You'll find it on that ledge in the cave with the rest of the ammunition."

I went inside and came back out with the gun, bringing enough cartridges for a load. Wyatt watched as I fed them in.

"When did Ben start letting you shoot his?" he asked.

"Since the first time I went hunting with him. I was nine then."

"Then I reckon you won't need any help from me."

The gun gleamed with blue newness. I lifted it and sighted along the barrel, feeling more at home with it from the first than I did with the Colt. Looking at the claybank, I vowed to sleep with it beside me from then on.

We dressed out the buck, salted the carcass down, and made a scaffold inside the cave to hang him from. Wyatt

went out for some mountain oak, and we built a small
fire and started the meat to smoking.

There was time as well before dark to haul in a fresh
log behind the mare. We split it with ax and chisel. Turning the flat sides down, we began to work out holes for
the pegs that would turn it into a table. Maybe an hour
before sundown, Wyatt stopped.

"We'll go out and shoot some," he said.

He set up some of the woodchips and stepped off
maybe forty feet and drew a line. I stood at his mark and
drew the Colt.

"Repeat what we went through yesterday," he said.

"Deliberate draw, don't aim, just point."

"And squeeze," he said, "like you're pressing a lady's hand."

I hit a chip on my first try. When the gun was empty,
he walked to the targets, picked each one up, and studied
them. Then he came back.

"You sure you never shot a six-gun before?"

"Never."

He turned back and looked at the chips once more.
Then he said, "You're going to be good."

There was no pride in his words, though. If anything
I heard regret. I paid it little heed. I guess I was thinking
I had made myself look good in his eyes. That was be-
coming more and more important to me.

"That'll be enough for tonight," he said.

I holstered the gun. We walked back to the fire. The
claybank nickered. I went to him and gave him a few
rubs about his ears.

Chapter Eleven

The work of getting ready for winter went well. I cut a large swath out of the grass along the lake. After several days, the hay was cured, and Wyatt took a day off from his work to help move it into the cave.

There was plenty of evidence of Wyatt's work too. He had put up another scaffold, and five deer were now hanging and smoking, the hardwood smoke turning the carcasses a deep amber to black. When we ran short of fresh meat, which we seldom did, we only had to go inside and carve a meal from a hanging carcass.

Wyatt had already begun to make the pemmican. First, he pounded the deer meat with a stone till it was pulverized. Then he worked salt and pepper into it and added the berries that gave it a sweetness. He then stuffed the mixture into deer intestines that he had scraped and washed. Hanging the sausages along the scaffold, he smoked them beside the deer carcasses.

We fished in the lake from time to time for variety. We were fishing once when Wyatt got the idea to fence off a portion of the water as a holding pen for when we caught more fish than we wanted to cook. We made the fence with stones, leaving the spaces in between too small for the fish to escape. The minnows could still come and go, so the trapped fish could eat.

When the leaves began to turn, we went out to harvest

nuts. We rode for miles to lower altitudes to find them—wild pecans, hickory nuts, and acorns. The acorns had to be hulled and bleached before they could be eaten. When this was done, we pounded them into a flour, which we stored in containers made from the soapstone from the lake. Wyatt said we'd cook them into hoecakes like cornbread. The nuts we stored in bins made by a circle of stones.

As we rode down for the nuts, we kept an eye out for berries and roots. We gathered the seeds of the sego lilly and the manzanita, both of which were pounded into flour and stored, something Wyatt said he'd learned from the Cheyenne.

The day came when Wyatt announced that we had sufficient supplies laid in, and he gave me a couple of days off to do some exploring. I asked him to join me, but he said he would stay behind in camp and continue to store firewood for the winter.

That morning when I was preparing to leave, he told me to ride to the west . . . never to the east. He didn't have to tell me why. I knew. Lafe Kennedy and his gang would come from the east, if they came.

Wyatt followed me out to where the claybank waited, saddled and ready.

"Here, take this," he said, giving me his compass. He asked me to check the rifle's load, and he checked to see that I carried plenty of extra cartridges.

"Keep an eye out for that grizzly," he called after me.

I spent most of the morning riding and looking. I found a cliff that overhung a stream and had hundreds of mud swallow nests made from mud hanging from it. I spent an hour watching the birds come and go, feeding their young and repairing their nests. I had fallen into the habit of talking to the claybank when we were alone, and I did a lot of that. Anyone nearby would have thought I was crazy.

From time to time I checked my direction with the compass. Out of the northwest tall phalanxes of clouds, their bases threateningly black, rode the wind across the sky. The temperature had already dropped, and I wore my fleece-line coat and gloves that Wyatt had bought when we stopped in Trinidad.

I had watched the slopes as the aspen turned from green to yellow and then gold. Now the slopes were riots of color. All that color simply increased the mystery of the mountains for me.

I followed an animal trail up a slope to a spring and decided to have lunch there. I gave the claybank a loose rein so he could graze, and, lying on my belly, I drank. The water was very cold, as though it came off ice. Winter, I decided, wouldn't be long in coming.

Overhead the wind stirred the aspen, shaking the leaves loose and turning them into golden showers that drifted down to me.

I felt a great contentment as I listened to the claybank graze and the wind caused the trees overhead to sigh and turn loose their loads, and I dozed off.

I don't know how long I slept, but an agitated snort from the claybank woke me. I sat up and looked at him. His gaze was on the meadow below, and his ears were thrown forward nervously. In the meadow I saw something I didn't recognize at once.

There was a patch of blueberries, and they seemed to have sprouted something that looked a lot like a huge, oblong boulder, except the wind was whipping this boulder's fur about, exposing the black underneath, and this boulder had huge hairy paws that swept the blueberries, bush and all, into a snoutish mouth. The smacking sounds reached all the way up the slope. Then it dawned on me that I was looking at the big grizzly Wyatt was so concerned with.

He was a magnificent creature. I recalled the mama grizzly and the two cubs Wyatt and I had watched feed across a meadow. They had inspired in me a feeling for their wildness, but that was nothing compared to this monster.

Easing my way to the claybank, I placed a hand on his nose and whispered in his ear. When he was calm, I slipped the Winchester from its boot. A rock at the edge of the bluff gave me something to hide behind and a good view of the scene below.

I considered trying a shot, but as big as the bear was I knew a bullet probably wouldn't penetrate his thick coat and the layers of flesh underneath. Maybe one of the powerful buffalo guns Wyatt had spoken of, but the Winchester was doubtful. I kept the rifle on him, though. If he spotted us and decided to come up to investigate, I intended to see what the Winchester would do.

He didn't rise up from his crouch till he had cleaned up the blueberry patch. Then he must have caught a whiff of us, for he suddenly swung himself upright and twisted his head about a few times. Then he growled, sending a rumble that rolled up the slope and bounced off the cliff above us.

He twisted about then, still upright, his nose testing the air. When he faced the slope, he stopped and let out another blast. His front paws looked to be ten inches wide, and the claws, though they weren't extended, looked vicious and long.

As I lay and watched, I had the feeling I was looking at something that didn't quite fit into my Kansas view of the world. This was a primal creature, a beast with the kind of physical power that had always haunted men, maybe the very men who had made the carvings inside the cave.

He didn't stay upright for long. When he went to all fours, he rumbled away across the meadow to the south. The grass was tall, maybe five feet or more, and the bear looked much like a haystack wallowing through it. He disappeared in the aspen on the far side of the valley; slipping the Winchester into its boot, I climbed into the saddle. I'd had enough exploring for one day.

Wyatt inquired as to why I was back so early. I told him about the bear.

"You were right not to try and shoot him," he said. "To kill that big fella you'd have to put a bullet into his brain through an eye or his mouth."

Still, Wyatt seemed disappointed I had come in early. I asked him if something was wrong.

"Well, I intended to surprise you, but you've come back too early for me to have things ready."

"Ready for what?"

"You've forgotten what day this is?"

"I must have."

"Your birthday," he said. "Come on inside. I've got a present."

Once in the cave he gave me a package wrapped in brown paper. Inside were three books. The title of one was *The Adventures of Tom Sawyer* written by a man called Mark Twain, whose real name was Sam Clemens.

Another was *The Last of the Mohicans* by James Feni-
more Cooper. The third book was *Treasure Island* by
Robert Louis Stevenson.

"That's new," he said, indicating *Treasure Island*. "I
bought it in Dallas off a drummer. He said it was a book
a boy would enjoy."

As I've said before, I wasn't much for reading, and
Wyatt must have seen the look on my face. "You won't
find these anything like Shakespeare," he said, laughing.
"Not that there is anything wrong with Mr. Shakespeare.
Your mother and I used to read his plays together. But
these are adventures a boy, even men, can enjoy, and I
want you to promise me something."

"What?"

"That you'll read them while we're holed up here this
winter."

I wasn't up to objecting at the time, so I gave him my
promise.

Fourteen, that's how old I was that day. I had become
so caught up in what we were doing I had let the date
slip up on me. A boy's fourteenth birthday meant
something special. In the West fourteen was considered
old enough to take on a man's work. Many boys had
made their first cattle drive up from Texas by then.

Chapter Twelve

Maybe in the beginning I was disappointed in my birthday present. But I had promised, and, looking at the thickness of three books, I decided I should get an early start if I was to read them by spring.

Mostly, I read at night by the fire, which, I noticed, Wyatt kept burning brightly when I picked up a book. I felt I was reliving the story of Abe Lincoln reading by candlelight.

I began with *Treasure Island*. From the beginning when the pirate comes to the inn to kill the old sea captain and steal the treasure map, till they left the island with the treasure stashed away in the ship, I was held by the story. There was some killing in the hair-raising adventures Jim went through, and I thought of Mace Cantrell.

I couldn't help but like Long John Silver, though he was a scoundrel. Wyatt was right. *Treasure Island* didn't read like Shakespeare at all, and I still feel a little guilty when I say that, for I learned to like those plays when I was older. Partly, I reckon, because Wyatt had told me how much Sue Ellen had enjoyed them.

Maybe I can be forgiven when I say that Jim Hawkins reminded me a little of myself. He went on his treasure hunt, and I was on mine, though Wyatt and I still hadn't had time to look for any gold. But I felt I had it over Jim. I had the claybank and Pa with me.

Reading about that treasure hunt got me to thinking more about Abe Scott's gold. Before I started reading one night, and before Wyatt went to sleep, I asked him when we might begin to look.

"Have you been thinking about it a lot?" he asked.

"Hardly at all till I started reading this book."

He smiled. "When would you like to start?"

"How about tomorrow?"

"All right, but as I've said before—don't have your heart set on it. Despite what Buckhorn said about Abe Scott, I still have my doubts we'll find anything."

My heart raced a little faster. I tried to keep my attitude casual, but I put more faith in Buckhorn's prediction than Wyatt did, or maybe it was the book. Somewhere along the way, I began to believe we would find gold.

Wyatt went to bed. I went back to more of Jim Hawkins's dangerous adventure among the pirates.

We began next morning at the east end of the cliff and worked our way back. We took our time, examining every rock and crevice. We came across places where stone had been chipped away, and Wyatt said it was the sign left by Abe Scott or some other prospector. We were looking for quartz, for without it you won't find gold. By the end of the day we had less than a quarter mile and were still well east of the cave. To the west the cliff stretched on interminably.

Next day we covered about the same distance, and we still had found no place where Scott might have found gold. We certainly had found none ourselves.

I didn't give up hope, however. I was following Jim

Hawkins through all kinds of trouble. Things never seem to come easy.

We had moved into the cave, and Wyatt was already asleep the night the bear struck. We'd been searching along the cliff for several days by then. The weather had turned colder, but no snow had fallen. Maybe the bear was ready to go into hibernation. Maybe that's why he came.

The first I heard was a terrible roar. The roar was followed by a scream that made my hair stand up. I was frozen for a moment, wondering what there might be outside that was surely looking death square in the face. There was another blasting roar, and then the scream again, and I knew it came from one of the horses.

I panicked.

I didn't think to wake Wyatt . . . didn't even look at him. My rifle leaned against the split log table. Grabbing it, I ran into the night.

The compound was filled with the savage snarls of the bear, but over these came the frightened, pitiful screams of the horse. With a sickened, sinking heart, I realized that the furious sounds came from the very spot where I had picketed the claybank.

The sky was overcast, and I peered in the shadows along the rocks. I was desperate to do something, but I couldn't just shoot at the sound for fear I might hit the claybank. Frantic to help, I pointed the rifle straight up and fired off two quick shots. For a moment there was silence. Then the sounds of the struggle started again, the screams of the claybank getting weaker. I think I would have plunged into the conflict then if Wyatt hadn't grabbed me.

"You stay here!" he ordered, and he swept past me to be swallowed by the darkness.

He fired off two quick shots and let out a Comanche yell that equaled a snarl from the grizzly. That was followed by a quick, short silence so intense it matched the sounds of the struggle. Then the bear let out a blast that filled the compound and climbed the cliff. Wyatt fired again.

"He's coming toward you, Wes!" he shouted. "Get down! Get down! He's coming out!"

I didn't have time to follow his instructions. Out of the darkness the huge shape of the bear rolled at me. I had only time enough to lift the rifle and shoot, aiming at no particular spot, just at that enormous shadow bearing down on me.

He swept over me, knocking me flat, and I felt the terrible shock of being slammed against the ground, my head whacking against something very hard.

I opened my eyes to some kind of rosy light. I lay there and tried to figure out what had happened. When it came rushing back, I tried to push myself up, and sharp pains raced across my chest. Looking down, I saw the bandages, and they had brown spots where the blood had leaked through.

I didn't try to move again, but I did roll my head around to see where I was. I saw the fire then, looked up, and knew I was in the cave. It was still dark, for no light streamed through the holes in the top of the chamber.

After a moment I tried to push up again. I got maybe halfway when the pounding in my head began. I couldn't stand it and had to lie down.

Then Wyatt was kneeling over me. He put a hand on my forehead. "How do you feel?"

"Tell me about the claybank."

He hesitated, and I read the worst in his face. Then he said, "Well, I think he might be all right if infection doesn't set in. The bear worked him over pretty bad. Tore strips of his skin loose and cut him up pretty well. I've sewed him up the best I can."

"Help me up, Pa."

"I want you to stay where you are. I think you got a concussion judging by the bump on the back of your head."

"I have to see my horse."

"He'll be there when you've rested more."

"No." I started pushing up by myself, fighting the darkness that wanted to close me in.

"Boy, you're as stubborn as a jackass. I oughta tie you down and force you to stay on those blankets."

"I have to see the claybank, Pa."

He was silent as I fought the darkness and pain. Then he said, "I reckon I understand." He stood up, got behind me, and helped lift me to my feet. He kept an arm around me as he guided me to the far side of the cave where the hay was stored.

"How did you get him inside?" I asked.

"I'm not sure I know. I just managed it."

"I won't have him put down," I said.

"Boy, you don't know what you want till you see something you love living in agony."

I didn't think of it then, but later when I recalled those words, I wondered if Sue Ellen had been dead when he got to her. I had an idea she hadn't been. Maybe he had to see her suffer.

Wyatt had done his best to clean him up. Still, his coat was smeared with blood. Kneeling beside him, I saw four places where the hide had been ripped loose, and where Wyatt had sewed it back together. There were deep claw cuts over much of the rest. The smaller rips were filled with salve.

I went to his head, knelt, and rubbed my fingers behind his ears. He twisted about a little and tried to look up at me. I held his head up and slipped my legs beneath it. There was a slight rumble in his throat as though he tried to greet me.

"You're going to be all right, boy," I told him. "My pa has fixed you up."

I looked up at Wyatt, who seemed to reach to the ceiling of the cave as he stood over me. Thanks was about the only thing I could think to say.

"If I can't talk you into going back to your blankets, I'm going to pick you up and carry you," he said.

I slipped my legs from beneath the claybank's head, eased him down, and stood up.

"I'm going to be all right. He is too," I said.

"I wish I was as sure."

"What about the bear?" I asked.

"He got away."

"He was hit, though."

"I think he was, though I can't say for sure."

"We're going to hunt him down, Pa. We're going to kill 'im."

He put his arm around my waist again and led me back to my blankets. I lay down. He went to the split log table and opened a bottle. Removing the cork stopper, he poured some of the dark liquid into a spoon. "Open your mouth," he said, coming back to me.

I did; he slipped the spoon in and turned it up, emptying the medicine over my tongue. I didn't even ask him what it was. I was too busy fighting the taste. That black-looking stuff made Aunt Mamie's castor oil taste like mint tea.

"I'm going to kill him, Pa," I said again. "I'm not going to wait till he comes for the claybank again."

"I understand how you feel, Wes. But you have to remember he's an animal. That bear was just doing what animals do."

"I don't care."

"If he's been wounded, and I think he is, he'll be doubly dangerous."

"You'll help me then?"

"We'll talk about it. Right now I want you to lie back and let that medicine help you sleep."

The last thing I remember was Wyatt's face. He sat at the table, his eyes on me.

Chapter Thirteen

When I woke, daylight was streaming through the holes overhead, cascading down to form irregular patterns of sunlight on the floor. I looked at the spot where the claybank had lain the night before, and my heart froze when I saw he wasn't there.

Alarmed, I pushed myself up. He was nowhere to be seen in the cave. I made a rush for the outside, thinking that Wyatt might have decided he had to be put down. In the passage between the cliff and the rock fronting the cave, I ran square into Wyatt. He was leading my horse.

"Whoa there!" he said, catching me. "I just brought him outside for a drink."

"How is he?"

"Better than I ever thought he would be. He's been up since daylight."

I circled the claybank and carefully looked him over. He twisted his head about to follow me with his eyes. His wounds had already begun to dry out, proving Wyatt to be a pretty good horse doctor. His coat had been washed clean of the blood.

"How're you doing?" Wyatt asked.

"Can we go after that bear today?"

"Well, I reckon you have to be recovering if that's all that's on your mind."

"Can we go after him?"

"He's wounded. He left a trail of blood. That wound will make him more dangerous than he was. Are you sure it's something you have to do?"

Getting close enough to the bear to kill him would put our lives at risk. I considered that, but something inside me wouldn't let me back down.

"I have to go after him, Pa."

"All right, but when depends on your strength. You didn't say how you felt when I asked."

"I feel fine."

And surprisingly I did. There might have been a twinge or two of pain across my chest when I first got up, but at the moment I felt nothing. Reaching up I felt for the bump on my head. It had reduced its size during the night, and I was minus all the pounding.

"I could go after him alone, Wes. It might be safest."

"No."

He seemed to consider for a moment. Then he said, "Well, you let me know when you feel up to it."

"I feel up to it right now."

"Come on inside. I'll look at your chest."

Until then I hadn't realized I had left the cave with nothing but my britches on. I noticed something else then too. There was no longer that winter bite in the air. "What happened to turn everything off warm?" I asked, glancing up at a cloudless sunlit sky that made the day seem more like late summer than late fall.

"Sometimes it happens," Wyatt said.

"Will it last long?"

"Who can tell."

He didn't seem exactly happy with the weather returning to warm. I would have known why if I had taken time to think. A deep snow was the barrier that would keep Lafe Kennedy and his gang out of the mountains. There were the Cantrells too.

My own wounds, just deep scratches, looked even better than the claybank's. Wyatt looked them over and put more salve on them. He didn't cover them with a bandage, though, saying they needed air to circulate over them.

"Then when can we go?" I asked.

"We'll wait till morning and decide," he said, "but only if you stay in bed and read today."

Thinking that wouldn't be such a chore, I asked him what he planned to do.

"The bear left a trail of blood. I'll see if I can't find where he's holed up."

"You won't kill him?"

"No."

"All right then."

We got started a little after sunup. The weather had stayed warm, a strange kind of warmth that seemed to have a suggestion of falseness about it, like words from a man you know is lying.

Dew hung like crystal on the grass, and the birds which seemed to have been in hiding during the colder days, were out. A rabbit scooted away. His coat had already begun to turn white.

"He's holed up in a patch of aspen," Wyatt told me. "It's going to be bad if we have to go in after him."

"Why?"

"Well, with the dead leaves we sure can't get in close without him hearing. Of course, if the wind is right, he'll know we're near long before he can hear us."

"Maybe he's come out in the open."

"I doubt it."

The bear had bled a lot, and even though the sign was more than a day old, I could still follow the brown stains.

We left our own valley and traveled through a narrow pass into the next, following a well-worn animal trail. Wyatt had once explained to me that there was no counting the years the path had been used to wear into the rocks the way it had.

We exited the pass, pulled up, and peered down into the valley. I was on the mare, who was a little nervous at being ridden, so I kept a tight rein.

"Over there," Wyatt said, pointing to a low, rounded shoulder covered with aspen.

They were old trees, their branches starting maybe fifteen feet up their trunks. They were pretty well spaced out, and smaller trees grew beneath. More protected, these still retained most of their leaves. The smaller, leafier trees provided the cover the bear had sought.

"Can't we get him to come out?" I asked.

"Maybe we won't have to."

"What do you mean?"

"Well, he lost a lot of blood. Maybe he died. We'll be lucky if that proves to be the case."

I should have felt relief, but I didn't.

"How're we going to find out?" I asked.

"I got close enough to hear him yesterday. We'll leave the horses behind and slip up there again."

"How will we know he isn't still alive even if we don't hear him?" I asked.

"Good question."

We rode to within a hundred yards of the trees, stopping behind a low patch of brush, and swung down.

"Check your guns," Wyatt said, slipping his Winchester from its boot and following his own advice.

I did the same.

The walk to the aspen was up a grassy knoll. Wyatt kept testing for wind, but if there was any I sure couldn't feel it. Instead, the sun poured down, and pretty soon I was sweating.

Wyatt stopped thirty feet from the first line of trees.

"Did you get this close yesterday?" I asked.

"No, I stopped farther back."

"And you heard him?"

"Yes."

"I don't hear anything now, do you?"

"No, I don't."

"I hope it doesn't mean he's dead."

"I know you want to take your anger out on him, Wes, but that's foolish. If that rascal is dead, we won't have to put our lives on the line here."

I deserved the reprimand. Still, I felt as I did, and there was nothing I could do about it.

We were standing still, our voices low as we talked. A turkey buzzard swooped down and took a perch on a branch of a taller aspen. Another dropped into an aspen even lower down. He seemed to eye something on the ground, and then he disappeared into the smaller, leafy trees. He came flapping back up in a hurry as a roar shook the bushes. Both buzzards flapped sharply off and joined a group that circled above.

"Well, we know he's alive," Wyatt said.

"What're we going to do?"

"I'm going in. You're going to stay here."

"That isn't right. We wouldn't be here if it hadn't been for me. I should be the one to go in."

He looked at me with an appraising eye. I felt myself shrink.

"You don't expect me to take that seriously."

"No, but it's still the truth."

"You keep your rifle ready. I'm going to try to kill 'im in there, but if I don't and he can still maneuver, he'll come crashing out. You have to be ready."

"I will be."

"You remember what probably saved you the other night?" he asked.

"I got down before he reached me."

"You remember that."

"I will."

He was moving toward the trees before I knew I couldn't let him go in there, face the grizzly, and maybe die.

"Pa!"

He stopped, and I didn't even know I had called out till then.

He turned back.

"Don't," I said. "It isn't worth it. Let's go back to the cave. We'll look for the gold. I expect he's going to die anyway, or else those buzzards wouldn't be hanging around."

"No," he said, and he stood there and looked at me.

"Why? It's what you said would be best."

"That was then. Now is now."

"I don't understand."

"Once you start out to do something you can't back out just because you suddenly see some danger in the doing of it."

"Why not?"

"It might become a habit."

"I still don't understand."

"You will when you think on it."

He turned back to the trees. A moment later he disappeared into them. I followed his progress by the slight shaking of the bushes.

Meanwhile, I held my breath and cursed myself for not having fully considered the possible consequences. If Wyatt was killed, I'd never be able to face myself again. I charged after him. I meant to face the bear with him or bring him back.

I heard a low, menacing snarl about the time I reached the first of the lower bushes. Then the bear let out one of his ferocious roars and crashed about as in a charge. Wyatt's rifle exploded, the snarls of the bear and the explosion of the gun overflowed the grove and seemed to fill the valley. The bear, crashing about, shook the trees like a whirlwind as Wyatt's gun spoke rapidly three or four times. Then the roar of the bear began to die.

"What in tarnation do you think you're doing in here?" Wyatt shouted when I stood beside him. "I told you to stay out there!"

"I couldn't. I had to see if you were all right."

I put my arms about him, pulled him to me, and held him for a moment. *Dear God*, I thought, *thank you for keeping him alive.*

I felt an arm about my waist, the hand of the other on my head. "Your bear is dead," he said. "Now we have to skin him out."

"No, let him lie there and rot."

Breaking away, he said, "No, he's big enough to get both of us a winter coat. We can't pass that up. We'll slice out a few fresh bear steaks as well."

I wasn't sure I could ever wear such a coat, and I was

even less sure of eating a steak from the bear, but I helped. I *was* sure of one thing. No selfish feeling of mine would ever again be the cause of putting a life in danger.

When we got back to the cave, Buckhorn Smith was there.

Chapter Fourteen

"I see you got the critter that messed up the hoss," Buckhorn said. He sized the bearskin up. "How big was this fella anyway?"

Buckhorn looked different. I tried to decide what it was, but I couldn't come up with a clue. He still wore the same buckskin suit. Maybe it was a little cleaner, but I'd never seen him when he wasn't dressed neatly. But there was something, maybe a satisfaction I didn't remember.

"Big enough," Wyatt said.

He was studying Buckhorn too, but I think Wyatt was wondering already what had brought Buckhorn to us in the mountains just before winter was to hit. "You're welcome here, Buckhorn, you know that," Wyatt said. "But I wasn't expecting you till spring. Now I have to wonder. Is something wrong?"

"Maybe he's decided to accept a share of the gold," I said.

Buckhorn gave me a look and then back at Wyatt. "Before we get into that there is something in the cave you oughta see."

He led the way inside, and before we passed behind the boulder blocking the cave, I noticed he had already turned Old Sinner loose. That meant he intended to stay the night, at least. I noticed something else too. There was a small, scrubby-looking pinto mare grazing alongside Buckhorn's mule and the claybank.

Buckhorn stopped just inside and pointed to a smallish-looking figure rolled up in a blanket. At first glance, I thought it might be a boy. Then I noticed the hair. It was very black and very long. Parted in the middle, it was tied off on each side and long enough to reach well below her shoulders. Her faced was swollen and covered with bruises. She wasn't sleeping, for I could see black eyes peering up at us.

"My God, what happened to her?" Wyatt asked.

"Beat to a pulp," Buckhorn said. "I found her a few miles east of here yesterday. She was half dead. I got some food into her last night and this morning and finally brought her around. I think she'll live, but she had a close call."

"Who beat her?" Wyatt asked.

"All I know is what she told me. She's an Arapaho woman. She was captured by a Jicarilla Apache called Guapo. She didn't like him or the fact she was a second wife. She tried to escape. When Old Guapo caught her he almost beat her to death. She still had some spunk left in her, though. She stole that pony out there and got away again.

"She speaks a little English, and I know some of her lingo." Buckhorn paused and looked at Wyatt. "I can tell you something else too," he said in a cautious voice.

"What?" Wyatt asked.

"Old Guapo is behind her. I guess he's intent on having her back. Now, I don't want to bring anymore trouble down on the two of you than you've already got, so if you say the word, I'll put that little Arapaho back on her pinto, and the two of us will vamoose out of here.''

''Where would you go?'' Wyatt asked.

''We'll head north and find some of her people. They'll take charge of her and get her back to her own folks.''

''Why would you do that, Buckskin?'' Wyatt asked.

''Well, I've lived some with the Arapaho. They're fine people, Wyatt. I've got some friends among them.''

''I don't think she's up to any more travel right now,'' Wyatt said. ''The two of you will stay here.''

''And if Old Guapo shows up?''

''We won't worry about it till he does,'' Wyatt said. ''Right now I better see what I can do for her.''

He brought out his salve and a bottle of whiskey, and while the two of them worked over the Arapaho woman, I built a fire and started cooking some food.

Buckhorn, seeing what I was about, brought me a sack. ''Figured you two could use a few things,'' he said. He turned the sack upside down and spilled out potatoes, a cured ham, several tins of fruits and vegetables, and a whole supply of tortillas.

My mouth began to water at the sight of the ham. I hadn't had fried ham since leaving Abilene. I decided to cook it at once. I served up fried ham, hash browned potatoes, and tortillas. We had peaches for dessert, and nothing ever tasted better.

I had forgotten that Buckhorn might have come for reasons other than to bring the food. He and Wyatt fed the Arapaho woman and returned to the split log table for a second cup of coffee. Then they began to talk.

''Lafe Kennedy hit town a few days back,'' Buckskin said. ''He and his gang of thieves weren't there more than a day before they were teamed up with the Cantrells. Old man Cantrell offered to pay five thousand dollars if Kennedy brought your scalp back to him. Kennedy jumped at it, but he figures he'll get a lot more when he finds the two of you. He knows about Abe Scott's gold. It's not revenge he's after so much as the gold.''

''He's not out to get Pa for killing his brothers?'' I asked.

''It's the gold. Kennedy never liked his brothers that much. No, he smells gold, and he thinks he'll find it if he can locate the two of you up here in the mountains.''

''How did *you* find us, Buckhorn?'' I asked.

''Yore pa gave me a look at that map. If he hadn't, I'm not sure I would have.''

''Then we still don't have to worry about Kennedy,'' I said. ''He won't be able to find us before the snow comes.''

''Maybe, but they sure are trying. They're sweeping the mountains east of here, gradually working their way west. They're being thorough. Maybe they won't get this far before the snow flies, but maybe they will with the weather turning warm like this. The thing is, the two of you have to be on the alert. Better still, if you've located Old Scott's gold, you should pack up and get out of here. I'd head farther west, if it was me.''

''We haven't found it,'' I said.

''But have you looked?''

''Not much. Wyatt doesn't seem to think there is any.''

''I expect he'll be in for a surprise then. I never knew Abe to lie. What're you gonna do with a fortune, boy, when you find it?''

''I don't know. Find someplace where Pa won't be hunted, I guess.''

Wyatt was sitting beside me. He reached a hand over and rested it on my shoulder a moment.

Buckhorn sat across from us. I could tell he liked what he saw.

"I got a bit of news about myself," he said slyly.

We urged him to tell it.

"Well, it concerns the lady who was once the Widow Crockett. You see, the two of us got hitched not more than two weeks after the two you had to hightail it out of town!"

"Well, I'll be darned, Buckskin! That's good news!" Wyatt exclaimed.

"I never thought it would happen for me," Buckhorn said. "I'd lived all my years alone. But me and the Crocketts had always been good friends. Lettie says she never thought of me that way till we walked into the store that day."

He looked across at us, his face filled with quiet happiness. I knew then what the difference was I had noticed earlier. I had seen that look on Uncle Ben's face.

"We're happy for you, Buckhorn. Aren't we, Wes?" Wyatt said.

"We are."

"But you shouldn't have left a new wife to ride up here. You should be down there in Trinidad enjoying Lettie," Wyatt added.

I agreed with that.

"I couldn't stay put, boys, and wait for Kennedy and that gang to slip up on you. Maybe we ain't known each other long, but I consider you my friends. I had to come up here and warn you to be on the lookout."

"Does he still have the same gang with him?" I asked.

"Sure does. I've seem 'em all—Bodie, Johnson, the Mexican Padilla, Frank Stoudamire, and Rudabaugh Reese. Reese killed a man over a woman the first night they were in town."

"Well, we appreciate the trouble you've gone to, Buckhorn. We appreciate your friendship too. I don't have to tell you how Wes and I feel about you. But I think you oughta ride back down to Trinidad soon. You got Lettie to think about now."

"Don't rush me off, Wyatt. I'll go, but it'll be when I'm ready. To tell you the truth, I wouldn't mind that bunch riding in here while I'm still around. I'd consider I'd done the world a service to help get rid of them."

We spent the rest of the afternoon searching along the cliff for signs of where Abe Scott might have mined his gold, with Buckhorn joining us. We were well west of our cave, but we still hadn't found anything.

From time to time, either Wyatt or Buckhorn went in to see about the Arapaho woman. I went in once myself.

She was sitting up, and her face looked much better. I spoke to her, but she didn't seem to want to talk. The claybank whickered. I walked over to him and decided to take him outside for a walk. In fact, I picketed him near the other horses and left him there till dark. With the bear dead, I wasn't afraid to leave him out.

Chapter Fifteen

The fact that Kennedy and his gang had reached the mountains left me rattled, dispelling any feelings of safety built up over the past few weeks when it had seemed to me Wyatt and I were alone up there.

I had been angry before and I got angry again. I wanted to be left alone. I wanted to enjoy the only time I'd ever had with Wyatt. But the feeling that Lafe Kennedy would find us got stronger and stronger.

I worked longer at my target, but when I thought of killing someone the face and eyes of Mace Cantrell flashed through my mind. Still, I practiced.

Wyatt tried to hide it, but he was worried too. During the day, we continued to work our way along the cliff, looking for Abe Scott's mine. His eyes were never far from the entrance to the valley, however.

During the next few days, the Arapaho woman perked up. Her bruises began to fade, and as they did, anyone could see why the Jicarilla called Guapo would want her back. Her long black hair took on luster as she put on some weight. In fact, her hair practically sparkled in the sun when she ventured out of the cave. Her skin was a rich brown and without a blemish. Her eyes, inky black, reminded me of the black-eyed Susans Aunt Mamie grew in summer.

But she was still nervous and scared, her eyes darting

about at any sudden noise. Her high cheekbones made her face look broad but they balanced a nose that on a narrower face would have seemed too large. When she smiled, she showed teeth as white as pearls.

In no time at all, she was up and about, taking charge of the cooking and seeing that the cave floor was kept clean, even taking out what the claybank dumped at night if she could beat me to it. She found the curing deerskins and began working on them as well, pounding the leather, even chewing on it, to make it soft and pliable. She worked on the grizzly's fur too, giving its size admiring glances.

A couple of times Wyatt took her aside to talk. He verified what she'd told Buckhorn. She told Wyatt her name too—Evening Snow. I thought the name fit her.

It was about then that I decided Wyatt might have some interest in her. They talked a lot together. A few times they went out walking. Just when I thought Wyatt might be thinking more about Evening Snow than he was the fact that Lafe Kennedy had made his way into the mountains and might be closing in on us, he surprised me again.

"We'll do a little scouting to the east tomorrow," he said one night.

I was surprised he wanted me to come along and said as much.

"It'll be a chance for you to learn some more about tracking. That is, if we find anyone to track."

"What about Buckhorn? Will he go along?"

"We talked it over and decided he oughta stay here in case that Jicarilla warrior somehow finds out where Evening Snow is. He'll continue to search for the mine as well."

I was beginning to wonder about why Evening Snow was staying on, if you want to know the truth. Not that I didn't like her. Her being there relieved me of any camp chores whatever, and I had a lot more time to practice shooting targets and spend with the claybank, who was well enough to ride again.

Naturally, I thought her interest in Wyatt might have something to do with it. I wondered where the two of them would live if they fell in love and got married. An Arapaho village up north or in the mountains might be a good place for Wyatt to leave his reputation behind. I kept such thoughts to myself, though.

We rode out next morning, and at the exit of the valley I looked back. Evening Snow stood before the line of rocks and watched us. Buckhorn, with an ax over his shoulder, was making his way along the cliff. He had bragged he'd locate Abe Scott's mine before we got back.

We didn't set out blind. Buckhorn had told us where he'd seen the last sign of Kennedy's gang. We expected to come up on them somewhere west of there. Of course, we were hoping they would have given up and returned to Trinidad, but with the weather holding so peculiar we didn't put much faith in it.

We went carefully . . . a little like a steer trying to graze in a meadow he knew to be infested with rattle-snakes.

At sundown we went into camp. It was nice being out there alone again with Wyatt. We were more careful than usual, though, building our fire on a floor of sand in a corner where high water in a stream had washed out a pocket. Wyatt seemed more inclined to talk, and for the first time I asked him about Sue Ellen.

He was silent for a moment, and I thought I might have overstepped. He had told me to ask him anything anytime. Still, I didn't want to cause him hurt.

"Didn't Mamie and Ben tell you about her?" he asked.

"Some, but they always said they didn't know her very well."

"I reckon they didn't. We spent most of our time in Texas." And then: "What would you like to know?"

"How did you meet?" I asked, just to get him started.

"She was a singer. She performed mostly on stages, but when times were bad, she sang in saloons. I'll bet that was something Mamie never told you."

"No, sir." And I just smiled, understanding something at last.

You'd have to know Aunt Mamie to understand why she would never have mentioned a thing like that. Being on stage wasn't quite respectable, and a woman who sang in a saloon was seen to be of easy virtue. It would have given Aunt Mamie some problems that her brother had married such a woman.

"Don't get the wrong idea about your ma," he said. "I don't reckon I ever knew a woman to keep higher standards. She put her foot down about my gambling, and I took a job clerking in a store."

I thought of the times I had clerked in Uncle Ben's store and wondered how Wyatt had managed to settle down to that.

"How did that suit you?" I asked.

"Well, it wasn't the most exciting time in my life, but

I was content. She was there to go home to. We did things together.''

''What was there to do?''

''We were in Dallas, you know. On Sundays we went to church. On Saturday nights there was always a dance. She was a wonderful dancer. Cowboys from a hundred miles around rode in on the chance of dancing with her.''

''Weren't you jealous?''

''No. I knew how much she loved me. I just stood by and beamed, knowing I was the luckiest man in Texas. We went to church box suppers sometimes too. Even after we were married her box still brought a hefty price. The pastor asked me not to bid, saying others might not bid against a woman's husband . . . that the church needed the money.

''We laughed about her having supper with some young cowboy who had just spent his month's wages for the pleasure of sitting across from her to eat. Probably, at the same time, he was too shy to speak.''

I watched his face, which had softened a lot since I saw him that first time in Abilene. The memories of those times with Sue Ellen softened it more. I had the feeling he had slipped back in time and might be seeing his days with her as something to cherish—not something to turn him bitter.

''Then you came along,'' he continued. ''I thought I wouldn't make it through that night. I paced the floor, hurting at her pain every time she cried out. Then I heard a baby's cry, a cry that might have come from some lost kitten.

''The two of you were lying beside each other in the bed when the doc allowed me in. He stood by with the lamp so I could have a good look. She beamed up at me, and there was no sign of pain in her eyes, just that look of pride.

"You had your thumb in your mouth, sucking away and grunting like a pig filling his belly. I picked you up and held you, and I understood some of what she was feeling."

I was listening so intently I wasn't aware of my tears till he stopped talking. Somehow, hearing of that time made me feel more complete, like a blank space inside me had been filled in.

He didn't tell any more, and I was glad he didn't. There was enough fullness in me for the moment.

Chapter Sixteen

The weather continued to hold. There was what Wyatt called a high sky and hardly any wind. I had the feeling that when it changed it would be for the worse.

All the color was now gone, except for the evergreens, and the treetops looked like bare claws against the high sky. Beneath the trees the leaves were thick, rattling with even a breath of wind, or when some small animal scurried off among them at our approach.

Just short of the deep pass where Buckhorn had seen the last of their sign, Wyatt pulled up and studied the ground before us. "See anything?" he asked.

The ground was rocky and hard, but I saw it, a rounded mark where a hoof had bitten into the rock. I pointed it out.

"How long do you suppose it's been since that print was made?"

"How can you tell?"

He swung down. I followed. We knelt over the print.

"It's still free of any sand," Wyatt said. "What does that signify?"

"That there isn't any wind?" I asked.

"There was last night."

"The print was made today?"

"That's right."

"They were here this morning then," I said, glancing carefully around.

"One was," Wyatt said.

"What're we gonna do?"

"Try to follow it since there's only one."

"And do what?"

"We'll make up our mind when we find him. We have to ride careful, though. We want to see him before he sees us."

"What would you do if we caught up and he turned out to be Lafe Kennedy?" I asked.

"He's left me no choice now. I'd have to try and kill 'im."

We climbed back into the saddle. I could appreciate Wyatt's sentiments. Lafe Kennedy had chased him across most of three states, and now meant to collect the reward from the Cantrells. What other choice was there?

We did a circle near the mouth of the pass and came on the sign again. This time there was a string of prints where the rider had carelessly followed a slight depression with a collection of sand for a floor. The tracks went north, and we swung in behind.

To the west was the series of narrow canyons and ridges we had just worked our way through. To the north it was the same. These appeared to be a formidable barrier, but fortunately the rider turned to the east before he reached them.

To the east a round-shouldered hogback blocked our path. Running north and south, it was covered with timber, with here and there a giant shoulder of rock pushing through. There was a fold in the hogback just to the north, and soon the tracks angled in that direction.

"He won't get through there," Wyatt said.

"Why?"

"Look higher up. You can see where it comes to an end."

"You mean, he's ridden into a box canyon?"

"Appears he has."

"We've got him then."

"Don't count on it. If we go in, there is always the chance he'll get us . . . if he's knows we're behind him."

"Do you think he does?"

"No, I don't think so."

"Then will we go in?"

He sat the black in silence for a moment and studied the entrance to the canyon. On the slope to our right a covey of quail flew up, the flapping of their wings sounding like a dozen drums beating fast.

"There's water in there," Wyatt said. "Maybe he's ridden in there to spend the night."

"How do you know there's water?"

"See that thick bunch of trees a mile or so in?"

"Yes, sir."

"They've lost their summer leaves, but they wouldn't be growing there without a lot of moisture. We'll find him somewhere near those trees. Maybe we'll get a whiff of his campfire as we ride in."

"We're going in then?"

"You don't want to?"

"No. I . . . I want to. It's just . . ."

"Just what, Wes?"

"It's that we may have to kill 'im."

"If we do, it'll mean just one less when they eventually find us, and they will, you know. If we don't get him now, we'll have to later. A man with any judgment picks the time that's best for him. That time for us is now while he's by himself.''

''Why didn't you turn and fight them before?''

''There was never a time when it would have been one-on-one.''

I wanted to tell him not to ride in there. I had an idea he would have backed off if I had asked, but I didn't. I guess I bought the logic of what he'd said about picking the time that was best for you.

We went, Wyatt leading the way and stopping from time to time to study the layout ahead, and he tested the air frequently for the smell of smoke. We weren't talking, and the only sounds were a slight clink when a horseshoe struck stone and the soft creak of leather from a saddle. I rode behind him, hardly breathing.

Soon after we entered the canyon we came to two large shoulders that extended out from each side and formed opposite bluffs. Wyatt stopped, and we stared into the bottleneck for several minutes. It was the best of places for an ambush if the fella ahead knew we were trailing him. Then Wyatt touched his knees to the black and we rode on.

I felt stifled by heat though there wasn't much that high up. And I was keyed up, so much so that the buzzing of a single fly about my face sounded more like a dozen.

Wyatt stopped and threw up a hand for me to do the same.

''Smell that?'' he asked.

''His fire?''

''Yeah. He's made his camp. Maybe we can slip up on him while he's cooking.''

''Will you ambush him?'' I asked, remembering what he had said when I put that question to him before.

''No, he'll have his chance to surrender.''

''What will we do with him if he does?''

''Maybe he'll be so grateful he'll agree to ride on out and give up on this business.''

I had my doubts about that, but I didn't voice them.

When the canyon widened again, we sat on the lip of a long, wide depression. Through the bare tree branches a little smoke rose up. Beyond the trees, the canyon narrowed again and curved. My guess was that it probably ended just beyond the curve. Between us and the trees was an outcropping of rock.

''I want you to stay behind those and hold the horses,'' he said, pointing out the rocks.

''While you're doing what?''

''I'm going on in . . . try to catch him napping.''

We swung down and walked to the rocks. There was a slight depression behind them, and we led the horses down into it, tying them off to the trunk of a dead bush. Then we climbed back to the line of rocks and lay across them on our bellies and studied the trees.

There was no movement, and then I saw a bush shift about, and there was his horse, brown almost the exact color of the fallen leaves.

''Where is he?'' I whispered.

''Don't know. I'm beginning to think he's farther up the canyon. Maybe he's up there trying to shoot his supper.''

Slipping over the rock, he began to descend, leaving me draped there and not knowing whether I was relieved to be left behind or whether I wanted to follow.

I followed his progress across the open space between

the line of rocks and the trees, relaxing a little when he reached cover, though the bare branches of the trees didn't afford much.

My rifle leaned against the rock. I brought it up before me and leveled it on the trees. Then, somehow, even though the trees were bare I lost sight of Wyatt. I spotted him by looking at the brown horse who was following his progress as he worked his way to the fire.

He was there only a moment before he began to move again. When he came out on the far side of the grove, he dropped down to his belly and seemed to be studying the canyon up where it twisted out of sight.

There wasn't much there to study—just a few bunches of tall brown grass, a few boulders, and a bush or two. Then Wyatt pushed up and ran the rest of the way, throwing himself to the ground against the cliff where the canyon made its curve. After a moment he got up and peered around the corner.

The shot rang out then, coming from the cliff across the canyon from Wyatt. Wyatt doubled over and fell flat. Then he was up and running. I knew he'd been hit, for he dragged a leg behind him as he scrambled back toward the trees. Then the worst thing possible happened. He dropped his rifle. Now he had only the Colt, and the man on the cliff had every advantage.

I didn't even know the exact spot he was shooting from till the second shot came. It kicked up dust a couple of feet behind Wyatt as the sound of it crashed back and forth between the rocks. I saw the puff of smoke, and then I saw the man. He ran from some rocks at the edge of the cliff, moving fast along the edge to intercept Wyatt before he could reach the trees, and he was well out of range of Wyatt's Colt.

The man got off a third and a fourth shot as he ran, and he was gaining on Wyatt. Then he pulled up, lifted his rifle, and took careful aim.

I brought the Winchester up, took quick aim, and squeezed the trigger. It wasn't an outrageous shot, no more than a hundred yards. I'd downed a buck at that distance once when I was hunting with Uncle Ben. Still, I didn't make it. Instead of the man, I hit the rock behind him. The bullet ricochetted, screaming as it cut the air. Startled, the man put his foot down wrong and fell.

He tried to grab something, but there was nothing there. Then he tumbled into space over the side of the cliff. He seemed to fall very slowly, his scream rending the air. Even at that distance I thought I saw the shock on his face as he realized what was happening. I hardly heard the thud, it was so soft.

I lay there a moment, my face pressed against the rock. Then I thought of Wyatt. Sliding back into the depression, I untied the horses and climbed astride the claybank. Leading the black, I rode around the trees to where he sat on a rock. Pulling up, I stepped down.

"Are you all right?"

"Thanks to you," he said. "He snookered me. I guess he knew someone was coming in on him after all. Good thing he decided there was only one."

He had corded his leg halfway up the calf with his bandanna.

"Is it bad?" I asked.

"It hurts like hades," he said, "but it's only a flesh wound."

He stood up and, with his arm about my shoulders, we hobbled over to where the man lay.

"Turn him over," Wyatt said.

I did, having to bend down and get my hands beneath him to do it, and when I moved him, I found myself trying to do it as gently as I could, though what difference it made then, I couldn't have said.

"Padilla," Pa said when he could see the man's face. "I reckon now his partner will have to team up with someone else or ride alone. The two of them had been together for a long time."

"Broken Jaw Johnson?" I said.

"Yeah. If Johnson ever finds out I killed Padilla, he'll come after me, and it won't be for money this time."

"You didn't kill him. I did."

"Well, don't you ever tell that to another soul. Let that bunch think he died from my bullet if they ever learn he was killed."

"Won't they miss him and figure it out?" I asked.

"Well, they won't believe he just ran off, but maybe they won't get curious for a few days at least."

I think he remembered then that in saving him from Padilla's bullet I had just killed a man. Of course, my bullet didn't hit him, though I had intended it should.

The thing is, I hadn't thought much about it till then. When I did, Aunt Mamie's face popped into my mind. I wondered how I'd ever face her with blood on my hands. Abilene seemed a million miles away then and Aunt Mamie somebody who didn't seem quite real, someone who would never be able to understand what I'd just done.

Wyatt seemed to read my thoughts. "I know how you must feel, if it's any comfort to you," he said.

He didn't follow that up, and I was glad he didn't. What more was there to be said? I had crossed over into a different world. In the crossing I had lost something, though I didn't quite know what it was.

"What will we do with him?" I asked.

"We'll bury him."

"Then what?"

"We'll strip his horse, turn him loose, and then go home."

I didn't notice then he had called the valley home. I thought of it later that night when I woke up and found that snow was falling, falling in thick flakes as heavy as wet leaves, and the temperature was falling fast too. I pulled the blanket in close around me.

I lay there with the cover over my face and thought of Padilla. Then I thought of Jim Hawkins. He had shot a man when the pirates attacked the fort. I figured I knew how he felt.

Chapter Seventeen

By daylight the snow had stopped, but the clouds remained, turning the world gray and keeping it damp. The temperature stayed down too; I rode with my sleeping blanket draped about my shoulders and beneath that the fur-lined jacket.

We still hadn't talked of my part in Padilla's death. I wanted to talk about it. I wanted Wyatt to say something to me that would allow me to rest easier about my role in it. I hadn't shot him, but without my bullet he wouldn't have fallen, and yet I knew he would have killed Wyatt.

I thought of something Uncle Ben had once said to me. "The average man just does what is expected of him, Wes, which is usually the best he can do anyway." Measuring what I had done against that, I knew I had done no more than I would have expected myself to do.

At about midday we stopped to rest the horses. Overhead the branches of tall blue spruce intermingled, keeping the wind off a little. An owl had taken shelter among the branches. He cocked his head and seemed to peer sightlessly down at us, either too blind or too cold to find another perch. Wyatt took some jerky from his saddlebag and began to chew it. I did the same.

"What you did back there is troubling you?" he

asked. I couldn't think of a response, and he took my silence as yes.

"If you weren't troubled by it, I'd be worried. But the fact is, you did nothing worse than good men have had to do for centuries. There are men in this world who practice evil. They don't live according to the law, and sometimes they force others outside the law. Do you remember the talk we had on our way out here?"

"About having to fight to protect yourself and what you own?"

"Yes."

"I remember."

"I guess it just sounded like talk then, but you know what I mean now. Padilla would have killed me. Then he would have killed you. What makes you different from him is that you killed to protect yourself and me. It's good you carry remorse. As long as you do, you'll do the right thing. Remember this, when you do what you have to do to protect yourself and yours, you gain nothing by condemning yourself."

"Is this the way you felt?"

"My situation was different. I was ready for trouble. I went looking for it. Still, in the beginning it bothered me. I'm glad I can remember that."

"But Mace Cantrell. You didn't feel anything."

"I know."

"But how was that different? You were defending yourself?"

"What I am makes it different."

"I don't understand."

"I've faced too many men. I've *killed* too many. After a while the cause doesn't absolve it anymore."

"But you're changing, Pa. I've seen it happening."

He was silent for a moment. ''Maybe it's getting to know you and having a glimpse at what might have been. And I'd like you to remember that I felt something in the beginning.''

For a moment there seemed to be that dark quality in his voice and attitude again. I wanted to say something to wipe it away, but I had learned a lot about him by then. For a while now that view of himself would be etched in his mind.

Maybe he was thinking of how near Lafe Kennedy and his killers were, and there might be little choice for us but to face them or run. And maybe he was thinking he didn't want to run anymore, knowing that even if Kennedy didn't follow there would always be someone else.

But the talk had taken my mind off what I had done, and the knowledge that I had a hand in Pacheco Padilla's death didn't bother me quite so much.

One thing did come out of that talk. Our relationship took a new turn. Whatever the road we were on, we were on it together. There would no longer be the pulling together and then drawing back in our relationship. Whatever was to be Wyatt Walker's fate I would share in it. I accepted that, and I think Wyatt did too. He would never again say he shouldn't have brought me out of Abilene, and he would never say again he should send me back there.

There had been some changes in the valley when we returned, some of which had been wrought in the cave by Evening Snow. We would no longer have to cut boughs and bring them in to sleep on. Using our harvest of rabbit skins over the past several months, she had made a fur pallet for me to sleep on, and she had turned the bearskin into a bed for Wyatt. There were fur-lined moccasins for both of us, and I had a fitting for a buckskin suit made from the deer hides.

Buckhorn looked on the proceedings with a smile of approval, as if in bringing Evening Snow to us he had solved the problem of our comfort during the winter. I began to feel he had at that.

But Buckhorn had more exciting news. "Come along," he said when Evening Snow was finished displaying her handiwork. "There is something I want to show the two of you."

"What?" I asked, my excitement growing, for I remembered his brag that he would locate the mine while we were gone.

He wouldn't say what it was. He just led the way outside and west along the cliff. Half a mile farther on he came to a stop before a narrow crevice. "Abe's mine is in there," he said, and his smile was enough to light up what continued to be an overcast sky.

The passage was narrow, but we trooped in. Maybe twenty feet in, the crevice turned into a cave with a timbered roof, and there were signs of digging in the walls and on the floor.

"He had the mouth of the mine covered over with boulders," Buckhorn said. "When I first stepped into the crevice, I didn't see a thing. Then I noticed where a rock had fallen in and left a hole. I began to lift the others out and opened it up. Old Abe must have meant to come back, for he left his pickax, shovel, and gold pan inside."

"Is there gold?" I asked, hardly able now to contain myself.

"Follow me," Buckhorn said.

The deeper in we got, the darker it became, and finally Buckhorn stopped and struck a match. We had reached the end of the tunnel.

"Look at that," he said, and he reached out and broke off a piece of rock with his hand and held it out to me.

"What is it?" I asked.

"Quartz, boy, but that's not the best part. Look at those seams of yellow, and the quartz so rotten we can pick the gold out with our fingers."

His match died out then, and we stood there in the dark till he struck another. Turning the brittle rock in my hand, I looked at the gold. It had the look of bronze.

"How rich is it?" Wyatt asked, taking the rock to examine it himself.

"Depending on how far back into the cliff it runs, it's plenty rich," Buckhorn said.

"Well, a third of whatever we find is yours, Buckhorn. After all, you found it."

"No, it belongs to you and Wes. I'm just along for the ride."

"What do you say, Wes?" Wyatt asked.

"He's our partner whether he wants to be or not."

"There you have our decision," Wyatt said.

That night we celebrated. Evening Snow, falling into the mood of the occasion, cooked up quite a meal, and Wyatt and Buckhorn doctored their coffee from the bottle.

I wasn't offered any, which was fine. I was already feeling good enough thinking of what we'd be able to do with the gold.

But even as we celebrated, the presence of Lafe Kennedy in the mountains intruded. Buckhorn had been told of our run-in, and now he asked for the particulars. Wyatt obliged, leaving out my part in the killing of Padilla, letting Buckhorn think the Mexican's death had been by Wyatt's gun.

We began working the mine next day. As mining goes, the work wasn't all that hard. Wyatt and Buckhorn took turns breaking off chunks either with their hands or with Abe Scott's ax and filling a couple of our supply sacks with the ore. When the sacks were full, I tied them off, took them outside, and tied them on the mare's packsaddle. Then, leading the mare, I deposited them down at the lake where either Wyatt or Buckhorn broke up the quartz on a flat rock using an ax. With water from the lake, they panned the loose stuff. By the end of the first day Buckhorn estimated we had five hundred dollars worth of gold. When we trooped back to the cave about dark, I carried several ounces in a small skin bag.

Everyone caught the gold fever. Wyatt cast off his pall and ventured to suggest that if the vein held out the two of us might travel even as far as New York and take in the sights, a place he said he'd never visited but had always wanted to.

I suggested that Buckhorn and Lettie might like to come along too. But Buckhorn, his eyes twinkling, said no. He didn't think New York was any place for an old married couple.

That night I lay on my pallet and went over all the things we might do with the gold. After the New York trip, maybe we could buy a ranch down in New Mexico Territory or Arizona. I had heard there were isolated areas down there where men could escape their reputations. Wyatt and I would raise horses and cattle and live a good life. The solution seemed so simple I wondered why I hadn't thought of it before.

Over the next several days, we filled a dozen small skin bags with gold. We didn't forget about Lafe Kennedy, for the heavy snows we were hoping for still had not come, though we felt they were near.

Every day or so either Wyatt or Buckhorn saddled up and rode east to scout.

We seemed to have forgotten about Guapo the Jicarilla, till Buckhorn rode in after a day on the scout and told us he had found sign on the valley's rim where someone had been spying on us.

"It's not Kennedy or any of his bunch," he said. "There was a dusting of snow, and the man's prints were plain. He wore moccasins. His horse was unshod, and I trailed him south. There are a dozen of them. Unless I miss my guess, it's Guapo."

"Do you think his spy saw Evening Snow?" Wyatt asked.

"We can't assume he didn't. After all, she's been working down at the lake with us. I think we can expect a visit from the Jicarilla soon. What you want to do about it is the question."

"What do you want to do?" Wyatt asked.

"Well, I'm not for turning her over to him unless she wants to go."

"That's the way I feel," Wyatt agreed.

"Then we have two choices. We can fight them when they come, or I can take Evening Snow and head north."

"We still might have to fight them if they've seen her here. They won't believe she's gone. They'll think we're hiding her."

"Well?" Buckhorn questioned.

"I think Evening Snow should be told," Wyatt said.

"Maybe she'll decide to go back, but I don't think she will. She has a right to make that choice, though."

Wyatt had partitioned off a corner of the cave so Evening Snow could have some privacy. He called, and she came. Apparently, she had been listening, for I never saw more fear in a person's eyes.

"What do you want to do?" Wyatt asked her after he had explained.

She wasn't much for talking. During the time she had been with us, I could count on my fingers the number of times I had carried on any kind of conversation with her. Maybe some of it was her lack of skill with English, but there are some people who don't see the necessity of talking a lot. I think Evening Snow was such a person.

"I will leave," she said in a soft voice.

"You mean go with Guapo?" Buckhorn asked.

"No, I will ride north and find my people. I am well now, and my horse is fat. We will make good time. Guapo will not catch me."

"I'm not sure," Wyatt said. "I wouldn't rest easy thinking he might. Maybe one of us, either Buckhorn or me, should ride with you."

"You have work here. Your enemies could come and find your son alone. They would kill him and take your gold. I have ridden these mountains before with my people. Guapo will not catch me."

That seemed to settle it, and we turned in for the night.

Chapter Eighteen

The claybank was staying outside with the other horses at night. The first one up, I hurried out to check on him. The Indian stood just outside in the passageway between the cliff and the rock. I almost ran into him before I could stop.

He was dressed in buckskin, wore a blanket about his shoulders against the cold, and seemed as tall as a tree. He held a rifle before him. Before I could stop, the barrel was no more than six inches from my chest.

Actually, he turned out to be about six feet, but he was powerfully built. The large hands that held the rifle made the gun look small. Black hair, wound in braids, fell down each side of his face.

The sun was just rising behind him, and its reddish light enhanced the sheen of the well-oiled hair. His face was partly in shadow, making it seem to have been cast from bronze. The dark eyes held a glitter that reminded me of something about to pounce. The cheekbones were high, the face broad, the nose well trimmed . . . a handsome face, despite the threatening gleam from the eyes, a face that suggested some mixture of Spanish.

Behind him and filling the passage were a half-dozen more Indians, though not so impressive-looking. There was the strong smell of buffalo grease about them.

159

I backed up, turned, and found the opposite passage blocked by approximately the same number.

"Wyatt! Buckhorn!" I called. "We got visitors!"

Both materialized in the door of the cave at the same time, and they came armed, Buckhorn with his rifle, Wyatt with his Colt. They slid to a stop, took the situation in, and then flanked me, Wyatt covering one entrance, Buckhorn the other. Foolishly, I had come out without a gun.

"Inside!" Wyatt ordered in a whisper.

"And bring that bottle!" Buckhorn added.

I lost no time. Once inside, I buckled on my Colt, grabbed my Winchester, and then the bottle. On my way out I passed Evening Snow. She stood just inside the cave with the knife we used for butchering drawn and ready.

In the passageway the situation was still tense and a draw.

Buckhorn took the bottle. Uncorking it, he lifted it to his lips and drank. Then he offered the bottle to the front Indian but didn't give it to him right off. Stepping in among them, the bottle prominent before him, he led the whole group outside. Once in the open, he gave up the bottle to the warrior who had first confronted me— Guapo, I had already guessed. Guapo took a drink and passed the bottle around. For the moment they paid us no attention at all.

"It's Guapo," Buckhorn said. "What're we gonna do, Wyatt?"

"How well do you speak their lingo?"

"Well enough to make myself understood. I hear it better than I speak it."

"Then ask them what they want."

The bottle was empty by then. The Indians stood about twenty feet out into the compound, maneuvered there by

Buckhorn. At the same time, Wyatt and Buckhorn had positioned us between the Indians and the cave.

Now Guapo faced us with his followers behind him. Some were eyeing the grazing horses.

Buckhorn spoke for a moment to Guapo, who then spoke in return.

"He says he has come for his woman," Buckhorn translated. "He says she was seen here yesterday. He says he doesn't want to fight but he will unless we produce her."

"Do you think he means it?" Wyatt asked. "Maybe we can trade him something for her."

"What?"

"What about meat? We have more than we can use this winter."

"I'll try."

Buckhorn spoke again to the Indian, whose response sounded angry, and it went on for a couple of minutes or so.

"He says he'll trade the woman for meat and all the horses, including the mule," Buckhorn informed us.

I tightened my grip on the Winchester. I didn't think Wyatt was about to make such a trade, but even if he fooled me, I was going to have something to say before an Indian rode off on the claybank.

"Tell him not to be greedy," Wyatt said. "Tell him to take the food and leave the woman to return to her people."

"I'll tell 'im, but he ain't going to like it. We best get ready for some action."

Wyatt looked at me. I read in his look that he wanted me inside. I shook my head, and he let it go.

Loud sounds of protest erupted from the Indians when

Buckhorn spoke again. They shifted almost unnoticeably into a circle that had us surrounded.

"Get ready for it," Buckhorn said.

"No, tell him we'll let the woman decide."

"But you know what she'll say. She said what she wanted last night," Buckhorn whispered.

"Keep arguing. It'll give us a little time."

"Time for what?"

"I don't know, Buckhorn. Maybe the world will come to an end!"

Buckhorn gave Pa a look as if to say he thought Wyatt was suddenly demented, took a couple of steps forward, and signaled he had something else to say. The furor from the Indians subsided a little. Wyatt signaled for me to bring Evening Snow out. I went inside.

She still stood just inside, and she had heard. When she saw me, she raised the knife above her head.

"No," she said.

"Wyatt won't let him take you against your will, but he wants you to come out and tell the Indian you don't want to go. Maybe Guapo thinks we won't let you leave. If he knows you want to stay, maybe he'll leave and not come back."

She didn't budge.

There was no secret about the way she had come to feel about Wyatt. I said, "Wyatt wants you to do it." Still, she hesitated, and I saw fear in her eyes. But slowly she brought the knife down, slipping it into the rawhide string around her waist. Taking her hand, I led her out.

Guapo took a couple of quick steps toward her, raising a fist and shouting something. Wyatt stopped him by bringing the Colt up and cocking it. Guapo glanced angrily back and forth between Wyatt and Evening Snow.

"Tell him what you want to do," Wyatt said to Evening Snow.

She stood defiantly before Guapo as she spoke. I didn't understand her words, but her meaning was crystal clear. Guapo's face grew angrier as she talked. Suddenly he stepped in, took her arm, and shook her savagely.

"Wait!" Buckhorn shouted. At the same time, he stepped between Guapo and Evening Snow, bringing the shooting end of his rifle hard up against Guapo's belly.

Buckhorn spoke loudly in the Indian tongue, and Guapo suddenly seemed mollified. Reaching for Buckhorn's rifle, he stepped back.

"What did you tell him?" Wyatt asked.

"I told him he could have my rifle to go with the meat for this foolish woman who wouldn't stay at home."

"And?"

"He's thinking it over."

Guapo studied the rifle, hefting it from one hand to another, sighting along the barrel. Then he studied Evening Snow. "I trade," he said and turned away.

"Get the meat!" Buckhorn said.

Wyatt and I brought out two sides of deer meat and passed them to a couple of Guapo's men, who stepped forward. Then we watched as the Indians walked across the compound to their ponies, mounted, and rode away, Guapo carrying Buckhorn's rifle over his head.

"Will they be back?" I asked.

"No, Guapo has given his word on the trade," Buckhorn said. "He'll honor it."

"But what about your rifle?" Wyatt asked.

"I'll buy me a new one with some of that gold."

The others went back inside. I went to see the claybank.

Chapter Nineteen

Later that day Buckhorn and I rode south to make sure the Jicarilla weren't skulking about. We followed their trail about ten miles. When we turned back, the sign was still heading toward the southern half of the San Juans.

On the ride back Buckhorn talked of the continuous war that had existed between whites and Indian almost from the first white settlements. He talked of his own experiences as well. It was evident that he recalled fondly his time among the Indians, and that he was saddened by the rapid dwindling of their civilizations.

"Men oughta be able to get along with each no matter the color of their skins or their backgrounds," he said.

"Will it ever be better, Buckhorn?"

"There is a peculiar thing about the human race, young'un. Every man thinks his view of the world is the right one. He thinks his way of doing things is the best. Any man who doesn't look like him and doesn't do things the way he does is inferior and doesn't deserve the privileges he reserves for himself. Out of all that shortsightedness a lot of turmoil is born, a lot of killing is done.

"I heard an Englishman lecture not too long ago in Kansas City. He was over here to study the ways of the Indians. He had an interesting idea. He said that man is always evolving in his mind as well as in his body and his social ways. Says we even came from monkeys. Well, he argued that there would come a time when all men would be able to shed their differences and live together without fighting.''

''Do you think he's right?''

''I don't know. If it ever happens, we'll have grown a lot.''

I pondered that as we rode back to the valley.

Wyatt and Evening Snow were working ore down by the lake when we rode in. When Buckhorn reported that he was certain we'd see no more of Guapo's band, Wyatt didn't seem to be all that relieved. Buckhorn must have seen that too, for he asked Wyatt if something was wrong.

''Looks like the vein has played out,'' Wyatt said. ''We haven't brought out any color in the last several sacks of ore.''

''Maybe there's just a break,'' Buckhorn offered. ''That happens sometimes.''

''Maybe, but the quartz is thinning too. Look at those chunks.''

''Looks like it's turning to common stone,'' Buckhorn observed after inspecting several chunks of the ore. ''It's getting mighty hard as well. What do you think we should do? Give it up?''

''Well, we'll dig in another few feet. If we don't strike a better grade of quartz, I reckon we'll have to call it quits.''

''How much gold do we have?'' I asked, trying to hide my disappointment at this turn of events.

''Without scales, it's just a guess,'' Wyatt said. ''But I'd say we have somewhere in the neighborhood of $15,000.''

Dividing that number by three, it meant Wyatt and I would have $10,000 between us. It might not be the fortune I'd envisioned, but it was a lot of money. Plenty to buy that ranch with, and Wyatt hadn't mentioned the trip to New York since his interest in Evening Snow had grown.

There was no more gold. We dug for two days, finally running into rock so solid Wyatt said we'd have to have dynamite to get beyond it. We trooped outside without our spirits being low, however. Wyatt carried Abe Scott's pickax and shovel. He said both would come in handy . . . that we could use the pickax to break the ice around the spring when it froze over and the shovel to keep a path open into the cave through the snow when it came.

That it was coming was sure. Every morning the dusting before the cave was thicker, the temperature lower. The clouds swept lower each day too, the higher peaks piercing the fluffy black bellies as they passed over. And then they began to bleed, rain at first, then sleet, and then came the snow.

Not wanting to be snowed in for the winter, Buckhorn packed up to leave. Wyatt sacked up all the gold and told Buckhorn to take it down to Trinidad with him. He had written a letter to Uncle Ben and Aunt Mamie to let them know we were fine. He asked Buckhorn to mail the letter for him.

"I'm not sure I like carrying all the gold," Buckhorn said. "What if I don't make it?"

"What would keep you from it?" Wyatt wanted to know.

"Well, I can think of a couple of things. First, there is the weather. Those clouds might dump enough snow to trap me. Somebody might come up on all that gold next spring along with my bones. And then there is Lafe Kennedy. I might run into him and his bunch on the way down.''

''You're too smart for either,'' Wyatt told him. ''Wes and I will pick up our share next summer when we come down.''

''I'll keep it safe for you,'' Buckhorn swore.

I could tell he was touched by the fact that Wyatt displayed so much trust. I was relieved to know the gold wouldn't be in the cave when and if Kennedy came. If he managed to kill us, he wouldn't be any richer from having stolen our gold.

I stood by Old Sinner with my hand on his thick winter coat with Wyatt and Evening Snow beside me. Buckhorn climbed up. He was carrying plenty of food in his pack and an extra deerskin against the cold, a present from Evening Snow. Wyatt had offered him the bearskin, but the offer was refused, Buckhorn saying he'd ridden and slept less well prepared in worse cold.

We watched as he climbed out of the valley and waved at him when he stopped and turned back. He threw up an arm in farewell. Evening Snow and Wyatt returned to the compound. I stayed until I could no longer see Buckhorn.

Things were quieter with Buckhorn gone, but it wasn't a bad quiet. There just wasn't as much talking, something Buckhorn was good at with his tales of the places he'd been and the men he'd known. You had a feeling you were listening to history as Wyatt and Buckhorn talked.

Chapter Twenty

I think Buckhorn's leaving put a similar notion into Evening Snow's mind as well. Maybe Buckhorn's talk of getting back to Lettie made her homesick for her own family. At any rate, she announced a day or so later she wished to go.

Snow was still falling, but more lightly now. There didn't seem nearly enough to have clogged the passes, and the wind cleared much of it from the open spaces, drifting it against rocks and cliffs, making the accumulation seem even less.

The cave was situated especially well. The wind, blowing mostly from the northwest, carried the snow over the cliff and deposited it far out in the valley. If the wind shifted momentarily, the line of rocks before the cliff still afforded a barrier. As a result the compound had collected less than an inch of snow. The horses still dug beneath it and found a little grass to supplement the hay we had begun to feed.

That isn't to say it wasn't cold. The edges around the pool fed by the spring where we got our water were frozen, and the wind whipping through the rocks could numb bare hands and ears in a matter of seconds. Still, there didn't seem any reason for Evening Snow not to set out for her home if that was really what she wanted to do.

"I'll ride with her," Wyatt said to me on the morning Evening Snow chose to leave.

"Should I go too?" I asked.

"No. There's no reason you should have to make such a trip. You'll be fine here till I get back."

We were convinced by then that the Kennedy gang had been chased from the mountains by the cold. Any hunting band of Jicarilla would have already gone south as well. In fact, the idea of being alone in the cave was appealing, not that there was anything to shun in the company of Wyatt or Evening Snow, but I was nearing the end of *Treasure Island* and still had *The Adventures of Tom Sawyer* and *The Last of the Mohicans* to read.

I knew too, that Wyatt's interest in Evening Snow might be more than just seeing she reached her people safely. I could understand it. She was a beautiful woman, and there was something about her face that reminded me of Sue Ellen, or the picture of Sue Ellen, the eyes I thought.

They prepared well against the cold, packing more food than Wyatt thought they would need, as well as the bear skin and extra blankets.

The morning they left, I stood outside and watched. The sun was just rising beyond the peaks, turning the snow a little pink.

When Wyatt turned back to look at me, he looked twice as big he was so bundled up, and I could see the steam from his breath. I watched until they rode over the valley's rim and disappeared.

Inside the cave, I settled down with *Treasure Island*. I wanted to see what Jim Hawkins decided to do with his part of the treasure.

It was nice there. We kept a fire going most of the

time, but no fire alone would have kept the cave warm. The large boulder that blocked the entrance helped, but mostly the heat came out of the walls and the floor.

I thought a lot about Abilene the first few days I was alone. Soon half a year would have passed since I rode out with Wyatt. Christmas was on its way, and that had always been a special time with Aunt Mamie, Uncle Ben, and me.

But six months with Wyatt and I seemed like a different person. Though I'd always love Aunt Mamie and Uncle Ben, I already knew that I would never go back to live with them for good.

Such thoughts made me restless, and I put the book aside and went out to the compound. Darkness was coming on, though the sun was still to set. Behind the gray film in the sky, the sun resembled a light made dim by heavy fog. That was the first night I brought the horses inside.

After a week I began to look for Wyatt. I wasn't too worried about his being trapped by snow, though the dustings had increased in intensity. On the night before the eighth day I went to sleep unworried, confident I would see him ride in soon.

When I woke up, I glanced at the holes in the roof of the cave, a way I had of checking the time. Dawn had just begun to gray the sky. Pushing myself up, I looked into a face I'll never forget.

He wore a buffalo robe coat that reached almost to the tops of his boots. He was big enough without the coat, but its bulk made him resemble the size and shape of the grizzly we had killed. He had a fur-lined hat pulled well down over his ears, the fur inside, the outside just the inner skin of the animal.

Thick, bushy brows; hooded, piercing eyes; and a thick dark beard covered his face with the exception of one distinctly strange portion, the left side. In the middle of that bare spot was his mouth, well to the left of where it was supposed to be. Suddenly, he stooped and put his hands on his knees. His eyes had the look of an animal about to pounce.

"Who are you?" I asked, maybe hoping I was dreaming.

He gave what passed for a laugh, except it wasn't like any laugh I had ever heard. "Lafe," he called, "come in here and see what I done found!" His speech was muffled by the position of his mouth, but I could still understand him.

I knew at once who he was, for he fit exactly the description Wyatt had given of Broken Jaw Johnson, and he had called out to Lafe Kennedy, the one man on earth I had the most reason to fear.

I had a moment before Kennedy appeared. I thought of trying to scramble away, maybe try to hide in the cave somewhere, but Johnson seemed ready to spring on me if I so much as moved.

I thought of Wyatt and thanked Evening Snow for deciding to leave. If she hadn't, Wyatt would now be in the same fix I was in. But where had the gang come from? With the coming of the cold and snow they were supposed to be in Trinidad!

Then Lafe Kennedy loomed above me. He seemed to dwarf Johnson in size, maybe because the buffalo coat he wore was even bulkier and longer. Instead of a fur cap, he wore a battered Stetson with a strip of dirty wool coming from under the hat and tied off beneath his chin, a practice of cowboys to keep their ears warm. I remembered the face from a picture in the Abilene paper. He looked a sight more sinister in person.

A batch of black hair held back from his face by the Stetson and the strip of wool fell to his shoulders. The hair was continuous from his temples to his chin, ending in a beard that reached almost to his chest.

He appeared to have a chaw of tobacco in his mouth, and the jaws beneath the beard worked up and down. The big nose and his upper face looked chapped and red. Beneath bushy black brows, gray-green eyes peered down at me.

"This the button?" he asked.

Johnson made a noise, but I had no idea what it meant. Lafe Kennedy reached down, took me by the front of my shirt, held me in midair, and began to shake. I felt like a rat in the mouth of a terrier. Then he slammed me back down so hard I felt my teeth rattle.

"You the button?" he asked again.

"I'm Wes," I said.

"Wes Walker, the gunslinger's son?"

"Yes."

"Where is he?"

"Who?"

"The gunslinger?"

"I don't know."

"You better tell me, boy. You don't, I'll turn you over to Broken Jaw here. He just lost his partner. We found his grave. He thinks your pa had something to do with it. He'll take his mad out on you if I give him the word."

He hadn't even raised his voice, but that made his threat seem even more sinister. "You better tell me, boy," he said, bending a little lower, and now so close above me his foul breath sprayed my face.

"He . . . He left."

"When? Where did he go?"

"A week ago . . . to visit some Arapahos."

"That's a lie, boy. They ain't no Indians in the mountains now. They's all gone down where it's warm. Here, Broken Jaw, see if you can get him to talk."

Broken Jaw reached down and slipped his arms beneath me, lifting me like I was no more than chaff. Then he just tossed me up, sending me well over his head. I was on my back, but I began to flail the air with my arms, managing somehow to turn myself over in midair. I hit the stone floor with a thud, the air swooshing out of me.

Fireworks went off in my head, and my body felt as though it had suddenly been rearranged. But Broken Jaw wasn't finished. He lifted me again, but this time with a kick to my side. He kicked me again, and then brought his heavy boot down on my chest, grinding the boot heel in until the pain was excruciating.

The faint morning light in the cave began to dim for me, but I still caught glimpses of his face as he worked. The distorted mouth smirked with pleasure.

Then other faces appeared. Kennedy was there, the look on his face as clinical as a doctor's. Another had a face so youthful and handsome I was reminded of a clean-featured schoolboy. Those features, I knew, had to belong to Rudabaugh Reese.

There were two others—a bearded face so thin and pointed, it seemed out of place on a human neck, and the last, towering well above Johnson, was a mess of scars and hair.

I struggled to recall their names as extending circles of pain crept out from Johnson's pressing boot heel.

Frank Stoudamire and Big John Bodie, I faintly remember thinking.

They stared down at me, and I could see their lips move, but their voices seemed very far away.

Then the pain began to dwindle, but whether or not Johnson had removed his boot heel, I couldn't tell, because I seemed to begin to float toward some dark place and something in my head began steadily to spin.

Chapter Twenty-one

For what must have been hours I drifted in and out of the darkness. There were times when the faces seemed to float above me. More frequently it was just their voices I heard. Then I had the thought that freedom from any more pain lay in my making them think I was half dead.

It wasn't easy. Every bone and muscle inside me ached. My rib cage felt like it had been rearranged, my chest like it still supported Johnson and maybe another like him. Any deep breath shot pain through me, and I drifted back and forth between self-pity and anger, sometimes blaming Wyatt for leaving me alone.

Then gradually the self-pity vanished, and I was just mad. I wanted to smash them, get back at them for chasing us across two states. I wanted to fix them so they'd never kill or torture again. I imagined how I would feel when I brought destruction down on them. Still, I had to figure some way to do it, and they outnumbered me five to one.

First, I had to arm myself. I tried to remember where I had last left the Colt. Like Wyatt, it was my habit to sleep with it near. Through just a slit between my lids I glanced slowly around. I didn't see anyone, but I could hear them talking.

I began to search about with my hand, not daring to

raise up and look for fear someone at the table might glance my way. The only thing I found was a rock, a rock maybe the size of my fist, not much of a weapon, but I squeezed it and brought it in, hiding it beneath my blanket.

Hearing the grind of a boot on stone, I closed my eyes, leaving only a narrow slit, and became as motionless as the stone beside me. Then Lafe Kennedy with a torch above his head appeared, stood there a moment, and stared down at me. Then he turned away, cursing as he went.

They cooked, making free with our supplies. I kept thinking of how they had passed the whiskey around the night Wyatt ran their horses off. I waited as patiently as I could for them to eat, hoping they'd settle down to drink when they did. They'd sleep heavier drunk, and I would have an easier time, though what it was I would do hadn't come to me yet.

I heard someone move in my direction, and I played possum again. But they didn't come to me. Instead, they stopped at the hay and loaded up. Obviously, they meant to take some out to their horses.

"Frank, put that cigarette out!" Lafe Kennedy yelled. "You want to catch that pile of hay on fire? It'd run us out of here!"

"Ah, Lafe!" Stoudamire grumbled, but he dropped the cigarette and ground it with his boot.

My hand drifted down to my pocket. I had begun to carry a small tin of matches, copying Wyatt's practice. It was still there. I thought of how the piles of burning hay would send them running and clutched the box that held my matches, not thinking that I would be in the same danger.

I watched the passing of that day through the holes in the top of the cave. They cooked and ate, then cooked and ate again. I waited for them to bring the bottle out. From time to time, someone came back to check on me. Once, through slitted eyes, I watched Rudabaugh Reese's face as he knelt beside me.

"Kid!" he whispered, a hand on my chest. "Kid, you wake up and tell me where the gold is, and I'll help you get out of here alive."

I was tempted to throw myself on his mercy. He looked so young, so clean-cut. Surely he was someone I could trust . . . someone who would help me.

If the gold had been there, I might have offered it to him. Who knows how that would have turned out. I figured they must have found the mine and seen the signs of our working it. They would have discovered that the vein had quit. Maybe they had searched the cave for what we'd taken out. Not finding it, they would have another compelling reason to make me talk. I lay there hardly daring to breathe. Finally, Reese left.

As the day ended, I felt better. The pressure had partially lifted from my chest, and I could breathe without too much pain. I was hungry, though, not having eaten since the night before. My mouth watered till I drooled as the smells of food filled the cave.

The carousing finally began. As the bottle went round, either their own or Wyatt's, the talk got loud enough for me to hear, and they seemed to forget I was there. I lay with my head propped on my elbow and watched, unworried that I would be seen in the darkness.

"How much gold you think they took out?" Frank Stoudamire asked.

"No telling how much," Big John Bodie replied. "There's been a lot of fresh digging in that mine."

"Well, it isn't in the cave," Reese muttered.

"We gotta make that kid talk when he comes to," Stoudamire declared. "Lafe, you shouldn't have turned Johnson loose on him. What if he don't ever come around? You'll never know where that pa of his is, and we'll never see any of that gold."

Johnson! Where was Johnson? I searched the cave in vain for him. Was he on guard outside? Even if the other four drank themselves into oblivion, Johnson would remain sober. What would that do to any plan I devised?

He trooped in then, shed the burly buffalo coat, shook the snow from it, and tossed it aside.

"See anything out there?" Kennedy asked him.

Johnson said something. I couldn't understand the words, but I could read his face. Apparently, he hadn't seen anything but snow. He reached over the table and took the bottle from Stoudamire's hand. Lifting it to his distorted mouth, he stuck the bottle in, turned it and his face toward the ceiling, and drank. When he was finished, he passed the bottle to Reese. Reese took it, but before he drank, he carefully wiped the top with his bandanna.

"Get back outside now!" Kennedy ordered.

Johnson appeared to object.

"You got another hour out there," Bodie told him.

Johnson left.

The rest continued to drink, though they seemed to be slowing down. Finally, Bodie rose and stretched. "I'll grab a wink before I spell Johnson outside."

One by one the whiskey got to them. Stoudamire went next. A few minutes later Reese got up, threw more wood on the fire, and stretched out nearby. Finally, there was only Kennedy. He emptied the bottle, and when he got up from the table, instead of going to bed, he walked back and stared down at me for several moments.

Muttering something under his breath, he went back to the fire. He stood above it a moment, then went to the table, crawled up on it, and stretched out. In nothing flat, I heard his snores.

It seemed to me if I was going to attempt something the time had come. I still had only the rock for a weapon.

Maybe if I could make it to the fire, I could knock one of them out and steal a gun.

I pushed myself up, threw the blanket aside and, staying in the shadows, crawled along the side of the cave—and found my rifle! In the commotion of the men coming and going, someone had bumped it, sliding it into its hiding place. I picked it up and checked its load.

With the Winchester in hand and loaded, I felt better. My first thought was to get behind the rocks and start shooting them one by one where they lay. But how many could I kill before the rest were up and shooting back? And Johnson was outside. He could keep me pinned down in the cave forever. I needed to have them all before me and them at the disadvantage of not knowing where I was.

I took the matches out, eased across to the hay, struck one, and touched the flame to the dry grass. It burned hungrily. The rifle at ready in case someone woke up early, I snaked through the cave. At the exit, I turned and looked back. The fire in the hay was climbing the cavern wall, the flames already reaching to near the ceiling. Smoke billowed out, filling the top of the cave and roiling down again. Some would escape through the holes, but once the cave was filled with smoke, hours would pass before there would be air clean enough for a man to breathe.

With the crackle and hiss of fire behind me, I crept outside to face Johnson.

Easing around the boulder before the cave, I searched the darkness. Meanwhile, fire inside began to roar. How much longer could the outlaws continue to sleep in the smoke? Not long, for surely they'd be unable to breathe any moment.

Even over the noise from the fire I heard Johnson. It approximated the sound of a snore, except it was louder, fuller, more like a prolonged snort from an animal. I followed the sound to its source and found him lying before the boulder covered with blankets and asleep. I put the end of the rifle barrel against his temple and stood there a moment trying to squeeze off the shot. I couldn't find it in me to do it. If he hadn't been sleeping . . . if he had been engaged in some evil act, maybe I could have. Leaning the rifle against the boulder, I searched the ground for a rock. I couldn't kill him, but I could knock him out. I found one and drew it back. A firm hand grasped my wrist.

"Leave him to me, son," Wyatt said. "You take cover in the rocks out there."

Chapter Twenty-two

It was a little while before bedlam broke out in the cave. Smoke now boiled out into the night, and tongues of flame licked toward the opening. The horses, smelling the smoke, possibly seeing the flames, broke free and began to gallop about the compound. Then the first of those inside dashed out, Kennedy first, with Bodie and Reese close behind.

They turned the corner around the boulder and came face-to-face with Wyatt. There was no sign of Stoudamire, and I remembered he had been sleeping closest to the hay.

I knew I had to do something. Wyatt, facing three gunmen, stood no chance if I didn't. Kennedy made the first move. Seeing the enemy he had come so far to kill, he reached for his six-gun and fired at Wyatt. Wyatt stumbled, and I lost count of what happened then.

All I can remember is that I was working the Winchester as fast as I could. I saw Kennedy pitch forward. Bodie went down next, but Reese had slipped through and was chasing the horse around the compound. Then something exploded inside my head.

I came to with Wyatt's face only inches above my own. "What happened?" I managed to ask.

"Johnson woke up and took a shot at you. His bullet scraped your head."

"Am I going to live?"

"Till a ripe old age, and you'll die in bed."

"Are they all dead?"

"Kennedy, Bodie, and Johnson surely are. I think Stoudamire died inside."

"Reese is out there chasing a horse!" I managed to say to Wyatt.

"No, not anymore. I couldn't catch him," a voice said from the rocks.

"Get down, Wes!" Wyatt shouted.

"Your son has nothing to fear from me, Mr. Walker," Reese said. "You see, I rushed out of there without my guns."

"Come out then with your hands in the air!"

He stepped out, his hands high. "I ain't got no real quarrel with you, Mr. Walker," he said. "Never did have. Lafe just got me fired up over the gold. That's why I came along."

"You wouldn't have killed me if you'd had the chance?" Wyatt asked.

"Well, I can't say I wouldn't have and tell the truth. You see, Lafe would have killed me if he'd found out I'd had a chance and didn't take it. So you do what you have to do."

I waited. Reese had killed his share of men. If he'd had a gun there in the rocks, he surely would have shot both of us. Still, he was an unarmed man. Would Wyatt shoot him? I don't think I could have faulted him.

"I know something of you, Reese," Wyatt said. "I never knew you to go back on your word. What would you give to live?"

"My word never to bother you and yours again, and I'll add another provision."

"What's that?"

"If you ever need my gun, it's yours for the asking."

"I hope I never come to that, but there is something I wish you would do."

"What? Mr. Walker. Name it."

"Go back to Philadelphia. Join your family. Turn your life around."

"Like you did, Mr. Walker?"

I didn't miss the irony in Reese's voice. I wondered what Wyatt would say.

"Like I'm trying to do at last, Mr. Reese. Like I'm trying to do."

We spent the rest of that night in the passage between the cave and the great boulder. We had a fire, but we didn't need it for warmth. The boulder blocked the wind, and a lot of heat came from the cave. I slept that night within two feet of Rudabaugh Reese, a man who the day before had seemed to be an original member of Satan's own crew.

He left early the next morning, riding out on a saddleless horse, since all the gear had been burned in the fire. Wyatt and I watched him go. I didn't have the feeling he'd be going back to Philadelphia. I couldn't see him in a city dressed in a business suit. I knew of only one man on whom a pair of six-guns hung more naturally. He was standing beside me.

"Well, Wes?" Wyatt said.

"Yes, Pa."

"What shall we do for the rest of the winter?"

"I'm ready to leave the mountains . . . if you don't mind."

"Where do you want to go?"

"To Trinidad to pick up our gold from Buckhorn."

"Where to then? Maybe to New York City?"

"No, sir."

"Where then?"

"How about New Mexico? We could take the gold and buy a ranch to settle on. How about raising some horses and cattle?"

"I've seen some likely places down there."

"Where?" I asked.

"There's a river. It's called the Ruidoso. Its waters coming out of the mountains are as sweet as lemonade. The valleys are knee-deep in grass, and there are pine forests so thick the sun never sees the ground."

"Hunting and fishing must be good."

"God Himself stocked the river."

"We can be on our way today," I said.

"Well, there is something I should talk over with you."

"Is it about Evening Snow?"

"That and one other thing."

"Tell me about Evening Snow first."

"I've asked her to marry me. Her family has agreed."

"She's a good woman. Now what is the other thing?"

"I would like for you to return to Abilene, spend a little time with Mamie and Ben, and then you can join me and Evening Snow in Lincoln. That's the nearest town."

"What will you be doing in the meantime?"

"When we reach Trinidad, I'll go to the marshal. I hope to get my trouble with the Cantrells straight. After all, there is no reason for the law to want me."

"What if they hire someone else to kill you?"

"They've had time to cool down. I have a feeling things can be worked out."

"And then?"

"I'll head for the village where I left Evening Snow. I'll bring her down, and we'll be married."

"And have a honeymoon on the way to Lincoln?"

"Yes."

"You reckon Aunt Mamie will let me travel to Lincoln alone?"

"Wes, she'll take one look at you and know she's got a man on her hands. You can invite her to come for a long visit. Ben too, if he can get away from his store."

"I'll go to Abilene, but I need to ask you about what happened here. Did I kill Kennedy?"

"Why not just leave it alone?"

"I need to know."

"Yes, but you have to remember he'd have killed me and then you."

With a few supplies saved from the cave, we started down that day. I thought some of Abilene and my life there. Even now there is a music in my head when I say the name, a meaning too, the meaning from a state of mind when I think about Aunt Mamie and Uncle Ben.

It was 1920 when I wrote those last lines, June 13, to be exact, and late at night. Rising from my desk, I walked to the window and peered out into the night. I could see the Capitan Mountains of New Mexico in the distance. They were draped in shadows and appeared to be brooding.

June 13 was Wyatt's birthday. I had buried him five months before. I had hoped he would live to read my little book, but he didn't. He died outside facing the Capitans. Evening Snow found him collapsed in his chair. He loved the Capitans on whose peaks the snow remained for most of the year. He once told me he could see the patches of snow dwindling as the summers progressed. "Like a man getting old," he said.

We owed a lot to mountains, Wyatt and me.